FORGIVEN SIN

A NOVEL BY
DERRICK TAYLOR

Published by DTaylorbooks Publishing, LLC
P.O. Box 77871
Atlanta, GA. 30357
www.DTaylorbooks.com

ISBN: 978-1-61364-706-6
LCCN: 2012901280

Acknowledgments

I wish to Thank and acknowledge,

GOD,

My entire family.

CHAPTER 1

"Congratulations!" roars from a crowded living room at once as Sinclair enters her home. "We are so proud of you," adds Clair, Sinclair's Grandmother, when the rest of the group finally quiets down. "My grandbaby is a college graduate now." "Thanks Grandma," replies Sinclair, smiling from ear to ear. "Sinclair," her grandmother starts to say something, as she follows her granddaughter upstairs and into her bedroom, where Sinclair intends to change out of her formal clothes. "Yes Grandma?" "You know, your mother would have been so proud of you today." Sinclair stares into her grandma's eyes as they begin to tear up. "You are right; I know that she would have been proud of me."

"Grandma, can you give me a minute to change into some comfortable clothes?" "Yes dear," says Grandma. "Just don't be too long, because we are celebrating our first college graduate in the family." As Grandma leaves her bedroom and Sinclair begins to change, she notices a shoebox underneath her bed. She grabs the box and opens it to see what is inside. "Photos," she says to herself. As she flips through them, Sinclair notices that every picture is of her and her mother Cynthia.

As she looks closely at each photo, all of which brings deep memories of her past, she begins to weep. Angrily, she starts to fling the photos throughout the room as she looks up into the sky to ask God "Why? Why did you take my mother away? Why?" she yells in pain. As the angry tears begin to poor heavily down her cheeks, she sprawls across the bed and memories of what her grandma used to tell her start flooding in. "When things get tough and you are losing control, pray and ask God for help."

Sinclair's family is very spiritual. No matter what the situation, they truly were always a family of God. As she reflects on the things her grandmother and mother used to tell her, Sinclair picks up the one thing that she knows would calm her down—the Bible. One scripture she always likes to read is Mark 11:23.

> "Have faith in God. I tell you the truth, you can say to this mountain, may you be lifted up and thrown into the sea, and it will happen. But you must really believe it will happen and have no doubt in your heart. I tell you, you can pray for anything, and if you believe that you've received it, it will be yours. But when you are praying, first forgive anyone you are holding a grudge against, so that your father in heaven will forgive your sins, too."

As she finishes reading, Sinclair calms down and says to herself, "Thank you God." As she puts away her Bible and finishes dressing, she hears a knock at her door and a voice calling her name, "Sinclair!" She opens the door to find her favorite uncle, Pete, standing in the doorway. Sinclair screams, "Oh my God; how are you Uncle Pete? I haven't seen you in a long time." "I know, baby," replies Uncle Pete. "It's been hard for me to come around, ever since your mother passed away several years ago. But baby, I am so proud of your accomplishments. Your grandma told me to come in here and check on you, and to get you back downstairs. There's a party going on, and it's your day. So, niece, lets live it up!" Uncle Pete puts his arm around Sinclair's shoulders as they exit her room and proceed downstairs.

As they make their way downstairs, among all the noise and cheers, Sinclair hears her Grandma's favorite old school song "Celebration" by Kool and the Gang. Everybody is singing the lyrics to the song in unison, some a little off-key and some filling in words as they sing along. As the crowd sings and point at Sinclair, she smiles and joins in with her family and guests, enjoying a great evening celebration for her special day.

As the evening and the party starts to wind down, Sinclair takes a moment to address the group, "Thank you all for surprising me with this graduation celebration. This meant a lot to me and I will never forget this day." "You are welcome," everyone in the room replies. As she gives hugs and kisses, Sinclair's grandmother notes, looking around the room, "I guess, I should start to get this place in order again." Sinclair insists that she would clean up, so that Grandma can get some rest and relaxation. Sinclair's friends, Christy and Jana, agree to help out as well.

Christy and Jana are her best friends. They all grew up together and later attended Howard University at the same time. The three of them are also members of the AKA sorority. Christy and Jana are due to graduate this summer, a semester after Sinclair, due to not being as focused on their studies as she is. The two are more of the partying type and very outgoing and tend to think shopping and partying are more important than their education.

"So now that you are finished with school, Ms. Hart, what are your plans now?" asks Jana. "Well, to be honest, I really haven't given it much thought." "You mean to tell me that, with a Marketing Degree, you haven't given it much thought!?" Christy questions, feigning astonishment. "No!" "What about the plans we all had to move to Atlanta and make that our new home?" Jana reminds her.

"Well, I thought about it, but I just don't want to leave Grandma and my little sister here alone. They need me," Sinclair says. "Look, we have been in Baltimore too long and it's time for a change," Christy chirps in. "Not to mention that, with our sexy asses, we will upstage those bitches in the ATL and show them how we do it!" At that comment, the three of them burst into laughter and began to ski-wee to each other.

Overhearing them scream out the AKA sound, Grandma Clair enters the kitchen, scaring the girls. She reprimands them, "Ladies, you are doing that wrong. I am the original Mrs. AKA," says Grandma, as she proceeds to ski-wee with them along with some heavy laughter. As the noise finally deceases, Grandma turns to Sinclair, "Go baby; go to Atlanta.

The opportunities you will have there are far greater than what you will find here in Baltimore. Your sister and I will be just fine. You have to live your life and make memories for yourself," Grandma concludes.

"Ok Grandma, you are right," Sinclair agrees reluctantly. "Just remember to visit twice a month and call everyday and that will be fine with me," Grandma adds. "You have my word, Grandma," Sinclair tells her lovingly and they all group hug. After the hug is over, Christy and Jana scream out "Party!" "What am I going to do with y'all?" complains Grandma, as she walks out of the kitchen with a smile.

"Well that's the last dish done! I guess, that's our cue that it's time to go home," says Jana. "Thank you girls so much staying and helping me clean up," Sinclair hugs both of her friends. "Anytime," says Christy. "Just so you know, when we hang out again, you are buying the first drinks." "No problem, just make sure you give me your credit card and I will buy all the drinks," Sinclair replies, laughing, as she closes the door behind the girls exiting her home.

Heading upstairs, yawning and stretching, tired from all the celebrating, she suddenly hears her cell phone ringing. She rushes into her room to see who is calling her to find her boyfriend Kenneth's caller ID displayed on the screen. She answers the phone, very upset. "Are you serious!?" she shouts. "You have the nerve to call me at ten o'clock and didn't have the decency to come to my graduation or my celebration party. Are you serious?" "Baby, let me explain," Kenneth interrupts. "Go ahead, I'm listening." "I had to meet with agents and talk to several NBA teams about this upcoming draft in June. It lasted all day until I called you just now."

"This was the one day of my life that meant a lot to me and you couldn't come. I just don't believe you, Kenneth. You have been lying to me far too long and I just can't take it anymore." "Baby what are you talking about?" Kenneth asks, rather surprised by the outburst. "This is for the both of us." "No!" shouts Sinclair. "This is for you, because all you think about is yourself. Oh no, I forgot Camille as well." "Why do you have to bring up my baby's mother? I told you a thousand times that she and I are just friends. I want to be with you and only you. Trust me; I would never do anything to hurt you. You mean a lot to me," says Kenneth.

A brief silence ensues, interrupted only by heavy breathing emphasizing Sinclair's anger.

"Look," says Sinclair, "I am going to believe you just this last time, but if this happens again—and I'm talking about the lies, the lack of quality time, and the trust issues—I'm done for good." "You have my word. I love you baby," he says. "I love you too." "Well, I guess, if you are free tomorrow, I can take you out to dinner and give you a surprise I have for you." "That would be nice." "Ok baby, I will pick you up around 5 o'clock." "That's fine," she says. As they both say goodnight, Sinclair is still a little bit concerned, but hopeful that, this time, Kenneth is finally telling the truth.

After she takes her shower and puts on her nightclothes, she gets her Bible to read a few scriptures from Proverbs. One in particular catches her attention:

"My child, never forget the things I have taught you. Store my commands in your heart. If you do this, you will live many years, and your life will be satisfying. Never let loyalty and kindness leaves you! Tie them around your neck as a reminder. Write them deep within your heart. Then you will find favor with God and people, and you will earn a good reputation." Proverbs 3:1-4

Sinclair closes the Bible, looks up into the Heavens and says, "Thank you, Mother, and thank you God, Amen!" As she begins to get into her bed, she hears a light knock at her door. "Come in," she prompts, knowing that her baby sister Tiffany wants to say goodnight. Tiffany is eight years old and although the two girls have different fathers, they are very close. Tiffany never knew her dad and was only two years old when their mother died.

"I am so sorry that I didn't have much time for you today. With all the commotion earlier, it made it very difficult for me to spend time with you," Sinclair says, as she hugs her baby sister. Tiffany looks into her sister's eyes and says with a smile, "Today was your day and I'm not mad at all. But remember, when my birthday comes, you should make it special for me too." They both laugh as Sinclair says, "I have a better idea." "What?" "How about we go and have ice cream and get pampered tomorrow?" "Yes!" screams Tiffany with delight. "I would love that." "Well since tomorrow is a big day, we need to get some rest and be ready. Ok Tiffany?" "Ok," she replies, giving Sinclair a hug before they say goodbye to each other.

"Rise and shine my darlings," is repeated several times by their grandma. "What a beautiful Saturday morning," Grandma comments, hoping to wake up the girls. Sinclair and Tiffany arise from bed to the sound of Grandma singing, "What a Beautiful Morning." "Tiffany," she calls out, "Yes Grandma," the girl responds sleepily. "Make sure that you brush your teeth and wash your hands and face before coming downstairs!" "Ok," she replies.

With the smell of bacon, grits, toast, and eggs in the air, Sinclair can only reflect on when she was Tiffany age and how she, her mother, Grandma and Uncle Pete used to wake up to that smell every Saturday morning. Although Sinclair and Tiffany's mother never really was around much at night, she would always make time to show up in the mornings for breakfast. Despite Sinclair knowing how their mother used to behave, she never denied the fact that she was their mother.

Their mother was a junkie. There were not many drugs she didn't use. If it could get her high, she would use it. Sinclair was named after her mother and her Grandmother— Cynthia, her mother's name, and Clair, her grandmother's, were combined to form Sinclair. She was only fifteen when her mother died. It was much easier for Tiffany, who was too young to have many memories of their mother. So, she would call her Grandma, mommy.

As they all sit at the table to start breakfast, in comes Uncle Pete. "Hello my ladies; are y'all starting without me?" he asks jokingly. "Sinclair!" "Yes Grandma?" "Please, get Uncle Pete a plate." "A nice big plate," adds Uncle Pete with a big smile on his face. As Pete piles his plate high with food, he begins to eat without acknowledging God, as Grandma always does before eating. "Pete, if you don't praise God at this table, you will leave here with your stomach empty," says Grandma. "Now, say Grace Pete!"

"Dear lord, thank you for this food we are about to receive for the nourishment of our body. Thank you for the many blessing you have upon us, and thank you for blessing Sinclair to graduate from college. In Jesus name Amen!" Pete says, obliging Grandma's request.

After breakfast is done, Sinclair reminds Tiffany of the outing they are supposed to have today. "What are y'all doing today?" asks Grandma. "Well, Grandma, with the little tie I had for Tiffany yesterday, I promised her that I would spend the day with her getting pampered and getting some ice cream." "Awe, baby, that is so sweet!" Grandma says. "But first things first," Sinclair says. "I have to start applying for jobs in Atlanta if I am going to be moving there soon." "Yes you do, baby," Grandma agrees with a smile.

"What's all this talk about you moving to Atlanta?" asks Uncle Pete. "This girl has her own life Pete and I advise her to move and step out on faith in another city," Grandma explains. "And don't try to change her mind." "I am not. All I'm saying is that there are some crazy people in Atlanta. I mean some sick people. You be careful out there!" "I hear you, Uncle Pete," Sinclair says with a smile.

"Wait, Atlanta," shouts out Tiffany. "Are you leaving me? Mommy left me, Daddy's not around, and now you are leaving me too!" Tiffany cries and runs upstairs to her room screaming, "I hate this house, everybody wants to leave me. Why?" She slams the door and jumps in her bed. Sinclair runs up after her, calling her name. "Tiffany, come back, let me explain!" "Leave me alone," Tiffany shouts back through the closed door in a tearful voice.

"I am not going anywhere until you open this door and let me explain." "Are you leaving and moving to Atlanta?" "Yes, but it's more to it than that. Please let me explain." "No, go away!" Stubborn as she can be, Tiffany refuses to open the door and Grandma insists that Sinclair gives her some time to grieve. "Listen Sinclair, she has witnessed a lot in a short period of time. She just doesn't know how to handle it right now, so give her some time. She will get over it."

"Maybe I shouldn't leave, Grandma. Maybe, here in Baltimore, is where I need to be." "Look baby, Tiffany is only eight years old; she has her whole life ahead of her. You, my dear, have to begin your life now. There is nothing here in Baltimore for you. You have to move."

Sinclair stares into her Grandma's eyes, tears welling up in her eyes in reaction to Tiffany being upset. "Am I doing the right thing Grandma?" "Baby you are doing what you need to do and what is best for you." Sinclair calls out to Tiffany, "I love you," as she heads to her room.

As it approaches 3 o'clock, Tiffany enters Sinclair's room. "Hey can we go get ice cream now?" "I thought that you were mad at me," Sinclair says with a smile on her face. "I was, but I know that you still love me and now I will have a place to visit when you move away," replies Tiffany. "You can visit me anytime you want to," Sinclair reassures her as she gives Tiffany a huge hug and a kiss on her forehead. "Let's go get some ice cream."

As they are getting ready to leave, Grandma is standing in the hallway with a smile on her face, almost in tears, happy that the two sisters had reconciled their differences. Sinclair looks at Grandma and says to her, "Thank you!" She knows that it was because of her that Tiffany is back to her normal self again.

Sinclair and Tiffany are set to leave but she has a problem finding her car keys. She stares at Tiffany questioningly, as Tiffany loves to pretend that she is driving when playing with her dolls. "Where are my keys little sis'?" she asks. "I don't have them." "Grandma have you seen my keys?" "No baby." "Dang!" she shouts, annoyed. "Watch your mouth," Grandma yells. "Oops, I'm sorry, that slipped." "I bet. You're not that old for me to put you across my knee," Grandma adds with a smile on her face. "Go ask your Uncle Pete if he has seen your keys. If I remember correctly, he took your car to be washed this morning."

"Uncle Pete, have you seen my car keys?" "Why are you so concerned about that beat up little Honda Accord?" "Cause that beat up Honda Accord gets me from point A to point B. More importantly, I love that car. I had it since high school. So, where are my keys, so that we can go?"

"Here, get these keys girl." "Thank you, and thanks for washing my car as well." Sinclair and Tiffany head outside to the driveway, but Sinclair notices that her car isn't out there. As she is trying to figure out where her car is, she notices a new car where her car is normally parked. She turns to see Grandma and Uncle Pete standing in the doorway, smiling at her.

"Do you like it?" asks Uncle Pete. "Yes, but who does it belongs too?" ask Sinclair. Before he answers her, Uncle Pete brags a little, "That's a brand new Honda Accord, brand new off the lot." Finally, not able to keep her waiting any longer, he answers her question. "That's your brand new car." She turns around and runs to Grandma and Uncle Pete to say 'thank you'. "How could we afford a new car?" she asks. Grandma replies, "God is good, and we have been saving money for this day every since you were a little baby. Now you and Tiffany go and enjoy your day."

They get into the new car and back out of the driveway. She turns on the radio, tunes into her favorite station and is happy to hear the voice of her favorite radio personality, DJ One Time, giving shout out the graduating class of 1997. She rolls down her window, turns the radio up to the maximum volume, blows the horn to acknowledge Grandma and Uncle Pete and speeds down the street into the city.

As the two sisters enter the main part of the city, Sinclair spots a white Range Rover that belongs to her boyfriend Kenneth. She is surprised to notice a light-skinned girl with sunglasses on and long curly hair sitting in the passenger seat. "What the hell is going on?" she wonders, as she proceeds to park on the far side of the street parallel to Kenneth's SUV.

She witnesses Kenneth politely opening the door for this girl, holding her hand to help her out of the car. As the girl gets out of the car, he closes the door behind her. The girl seems so overwhelmed by his gentlemanly manner that she gives him a kiss—not just any kiss, but a passionate, romantic kiss. "That bastard!" Sinclair yells. "I can't believe what I am seeing."

Although very upset, Sinclair pretends not to have any concerns, as her sister is with her. As planned, they go inside of Shay's Salon to get pampered. Little does she know that Tiffany is very observant. "I saw Kenneth with that girl across the street. Why didn't you say anything to him?" "Because I'm with the only true person I care about. And that's you," Sinclair replies, indicating that she is done with Kenneth.

The two of them go inside the salon. "Hey Sinclair; hey Tiffany," says Shannon, the hairstylist and the salon owner. "Hello," they respond. "Girl congratulations on your graduation yesterday!" "Thank you."

"What now, a college graduate?" sounds from the back of the salon. "Excuse me," says Sinclair, talking to Precious, who always seems to get into everybody's business. Precious is known as the neighborhood call girl and a stripper, but still has the nerves to think that she is better than everybody else is. Sinclair responds, "I am going to be just like you and take all your clients." Laughter emerges from all across the salon.

To be honest, many guys wanted Precious because of her body. She was this tall 5'9 curvy brown skinned sister that could have been a perfect model if she didn't choose the fast life. She was so into what man's material possessions that she never really cared for any guy past a certain point. She was always all out for herself. Sinclair and Precious never got along. Precious was always very jealous and envious of Sinclair. She looked at her as her competition because she was very gorgeous, with long hair. The only guy that Sinclair ever dated was Kenneth, as they were together since high school.

After the laughter finally calms down, Precious responds, "I already had your client," referring to Kenneth. "Since I can't taste myself, tell me how I taste," she adds, hinting that she and Kenneth had sex. Sinclair responds, "Soap and water trick." Laughter emerges again in the salon.

"Stop it, ladies!" Shannon yells. "Respect each other or leave my shop." "I'm sorry," Sinclair apologizes to Shannon before sitting in the chair to get her hair done. "What can I do for you?" asks Shannon, referring to the style Sinclair wants her hair in. Just as she begins to say something, Precious bursts out, "No matter what that bitch gets, it still want do her any good."

"Get out of my shop, Precious!" yells Shannon. "You have no respect for others. I don't want you back in my shop until you learn how to act appropriately." "Whatever," Precious responds as she leaves the salon, slamming the door behind her. "By the way, your man is next door. I will go and pay him a visit, as he is with my girl now," she adds, looking defiantly at Sinclair. "Bye ladies," she says with a smirk on her face.

"That girl is going to get what she deserves one day. Sleeping with men for money and using them cannot bring anything good. I am going to laugh my butt off when that day comes," says Sinclair. "Don't speak badly about her. That's not good. Never wish anything bad on anybody, no matter what they have done to you," advises Shannon.

"So what is the plan now that you have graduated?" "She is moving to Atlanta," shouts Tiffany. "Atlanta!" emerges from the salon. "Why Atlanta?" ask one of the salon's clients. "Because of the job opportunities I will have there." "Couldn't you have just move about thirty minutes to D.C. instead of going all the way to Atlanta?" asks Shannon.

"I just wanted to get far away from home. I mean, I do have some good memories here, but most are sad. In addition, my grandma reassured me that it's time for a change and that I needed to get away." "Well, Grandma knows best," Shannon adds, nodding. After several hours in the salon, the sisters finally have their hair done. "Ok ladies, you're all done. Tiffany your hair looks so pretty," says Shannon. "I am so proud of you, Sinclair. You make sure that, when you get to Atlanta and get settled in, you call me. If you need anything, don't hesitate to ask me," she says. "My only concern now is who's going to do my hair?" says Sinclair.

As they laugh and hug, Sinclair asks, "How much do I owe you?" Shannon replies, "Baby this is your graduation present from me to you." "Thank you." As they are getting ready to leave, Tiffany runs over a gives Shannon a hug and tells her, "I love you." "I love you too, Tiffany." Sinclair and Tiffany exit the salon, but Sinclair has not forgotten about her boyfriend Kenneth. The time is now 6 o'clock and she and Kenneth had plans for the evening. On the way to her car, she calls Kenneth's cell phone; not knowing if would answer or not. Kenneth answers.

"Hello Baby, how are you?" he greets her. "Where are you?" "Just with my sister," she says. "Are we still on for today?" she asks. "Well baby, if we are, it will have to be later tonight." "Why?" "Because, I'm out with an agent; he wants to represent me." "Oh really?" she responds. "What, you don't believe me? I told you that I would never lie to you again. You can trust me."

What Kenneth does not know is that Sinclair already knows where he is. She decides that it is the best to just keep playing along with him, listening to every lie he is telling her. She knows in her heart that, this time, she is done with him. Precious obviously chose not to let Kenneth know where Sinclair was. It could be deliberate, or because she was getting attention from the many men in the Pool Hall, it simply never crossed her mind.

Still on the phone with him, Sinclair says to him, "I trust you, no more than I trust your agent," referring to the girl he is with at the Pool Hall. "What's that's supposed to mean?" "Never mind, you do you and I will do me." "Whatever," he retorts. "I will call you when I'm done. Bye." With that, he hangs up on her.

As Sinclair puts her phone away angrily, Tiffany reminds her about the ice cream. "What about the ice cream?" "Oh yes, I almost forgot," she replies. "Let's go and get some ice cream." The two of them go into Baskin and Robbins for some ice cream together.

As they are having their ice cream, Sinclair gets a phone call. It's Christy. "Hey girl, where are you?" she asks. "Tiffany and I are at Palace Place."

Palace Place is an area where many shops and restaurants are located. Every weekend many people come there to relax and spend their weekends shopping and eating. It's a place mainly where the college students hang out.

"What are y'all doing at Palace Place?" "I wanted to bring Tiffany down here because I promised to get her hair done and buy some ice cream," Sinclair replies. "Girl, you are going to spoil that little sister of yours," Christy comments, laughing. "Guess who I just saw going into the Pool Hall?" "Who, girl? Tell me!" "Kenneth," she responds. "Ok. What is that supposed to mean?" "He was not by himself either." "Who was he with?" "Some light-skinned girl." "What?" Christy shouts. "You are kidding right?" "Not at all!" "Did he see you?" "No," Sinclair replies, adding, "He doesn't even know that I'm out here. But Precious saw me in the salon." "Who"? "Fake ass Precious!"

"We had it out in the salon and Shannon told her ass to get out." "Good for her ass," says Christy. "Look girl, you and

Tiffany just stay where you are, because Jana and I are ten minutes away." "Ok girl, y'all hurry up." "Who was that?" asks Tiffany, as Sinclair hangs up. "That was Christy. She and Jana are on their way over here."

It's now 7 o'clock and Christy and Jana are just making it to Palace Place. "Girl what took y'all so long?" Sinclair asks. "A flat tire," the girls respond in unison. "We had to wait for AAA to get to us and you know how long that wait can be," Christy adds, referring to the time when they were all in Sinclair's old Honda Accord and had a flat tire.

"Yes I remember many times when we were left on the side of the road waiting for AAA in that car." They all laugh, as Sinclair starts recounting some of those times. "One thing that I do know is that we will not be waiting on the side of the highway any time soon." "Why do you say that?" ask Christy and Jana. "Because she has a new car now!" Tiffany shouts out. "What new car?" "Look," Tiffany yells, pointing to the car, "the silver one."

The girls scream out loud, very happy for their friend. Christy says to Sinclair, "We have to paint the town red tonight." "You know it girl," replies Sinclair. "We are already dressed and we are already out, your hair is looking great, and not mention that you have two reasons to celebrate," Jana chips in. "The first is your graduation and the second is your breakup with Kenneth," elaborates Christy. "You are right. I am a free woman," Sinclair agrees. "One more reason is that you are moving to Atlanta soon," says Jana. "You are right girls, let's have some fun tonight." "What about Tiffany?

We have to take her home and that's about 20 minutes away," says Sinclair. "Let's move on then!"

Christy and Jana decide that they are going to leave their car they came in and all will just ride in Sinclair's new car. As the girls are loading into the car, Uncle Pete pulls up. Because the girls were gone for nearly all day and Grandma had prepared dinner, Uncle Pete decided to come and look for them.

"Uncle Pete, Uncle Pete," the girls scream. Pete hits his breaks. "What's wrong?" he asks. "Nothing, we were on our back to bring Tiffany home because it was getting late for her." "I know," he says. "Your grandmother wanted me to come and look for y'all. I didn't even notice your new car. I had forgotten all about it and was looking for your old car," he says with a laugh. "You mean the one you are driving," says Sinclair. "Uncle Pete is getting old and my memory is beginning to slip," he jokes, laughing aloud.

"Can you do us a huge favor Uncle Pete?" the girls ask. "Can Tiffany ride back home with you because we are going to stay out a little bit and celebrate some more? Please." the girls beg. "Yes, no problem," he replies. "Just make sure y'all are very careful and don't be drinking and driving," he reminds them. "We promise that we will behave ourselves." Sinclair responds, rolling her eyes. As Uncle Pete and Tiffany drive away, the start planning their night out.

CHAPTER 2

Sinclair, Christy, and Jana enter the Pool Hall. The Pool Hall is the spot to be on Saturday nights in Baltimore. As the girls enter, they are amazed to see so many people already there. "Wow!" says Jana. "I've never seen so many people in one spot ever." "Neither do I," Sinclair and Christy agree.

The DJ is playing "Set it Off" as the girls witness a crowd of people doing the bus electric slide. "Damn, they are doing my shit!" says Christy, throwing her hands in the air and shaking her ass, trying to get some attention from the many men in the crowd. As the girls make it across the room, Jana stops a group of young ladies. "Hey, excuse me, but why is it so crowded tonight?" The ladies respond, "Robert is throwing a party here tonight." With confused look on her face, Jana responds, "Robert who?" "Robert Brown, you know the guy that plays for the Washington Redskins," the girl replies, "He and a bunch of his teammates are here tonight, celebrating."

Christy's and Jana's eyes are huge because they can smell the money in the air. "I am going to get me a football player tonight," says Christy. "You are definitely not by yourself," says Jana. Sinclair stares at them both, smiling. "Gold diggers," she teases them, laughing as they continue to make it across the Pool Hall.

As the girls notice some empty seats at the bar, they rush to sit down and have some drinks. Still hyped about her song, Christy is still showing off her ass, singing the lyrics to the song, as if she already had too many drinks. "Girl that's one song that will never get old," she says out loud. "There are some fine ass brothers in here," adds Jana.

As they are looking through the crowd of people, Sinclair notices Kenneth playing a game of pool in the far corner of the Pool Hall. She notices that he is with the same girl she saw him with earlier in the day. Pointing in the direction of Kenneth and the girl, she alerts Christy and Jana. "There goes Kenneth and that hoe I saw him with earlier. I ought to go over there and snatch that weave out of her head."

"There's no reason to cause a scene," says Christy. "Moreover, that bitch doesn't have anything on you! So girl, don't waste your night worrying about no damn Kenneth and that bitch he is with." "Please don't blow my high tonight," shouts Jana.

The girls are waiting patiently to get a drink from the bar. The bartender comes up to them with a bucket containing a bottle of Moet and three glasses. "We didn't order any Moet," say Sinclair to the bartender. "I know, this is from the gentleman sitting across the bar," he replies. "Well, tell him that we said 'thank you, but no thank you'," Sinclair replies. "What the hell are you talking about?" objects Jana. "He is a total stranger." "That's less money that we have to spend tonight buying drinks!" Objects Christy. "Thank you," Jana says to the bartender as she accepts the drink from the gentleman across the bar. "Tell them that we said 'thank you.'"

Despite not wanting to accept the offer, Sinclair joins Christy and Jana and takes a glass of Moet. They toast in the air to a new beginning. Sinclair and Christy sip on their drink, but Jana quickly downs hers in one gulp, refilling again and again. "Damn Jana, are you thirsty?" says Christy. "You act as if you are in great rush." "Yes," agrees Sinclair. "You need to slow down before we're dragging your butt out this club tonight." "Don't worry about me bitches, it's on tonight. I am going to enjoy this night and meet my man in here." "In the Pool Hall?" shouts Christy. "Girl, all these niggas in here are looking for a one night stand." I will be getting me a ball player tonight," Jana says with a slight slur in her voice.

Sinclair and Christy are shocked to see Jana acting this way. Jana has never been irresponsible, but they realize that she has a stubborn attitude and they have no control over what she does. AS the song "Set it Off" comes to an end, the DJ chooses to play another old school hit, "Break 'Em Off Something" by Master P. As the song plays, the crowd starts to sing the lyrics.

Hustler, baller, gangster, cap pillar, who I be, your neigh-borhood drug dealer, a young nigga that's 'bout it 'bout it, I mean, these No Limit Soldiers, we get rowdy.

The fact is that there are actual drug dealers in the Pool Hall that night, which seems to be a regular spot for the dope boys on a Saturday night. As Jana continues to enjoy the Moet that was sent to them, she calls the bartender over. "Excuse me please, but can you give me and my girls each a shot of Tequila?" "With or without salt?" he replies. "With salt"!

"Jana, do you think you can handle any more drinking?" Christy asks her worriedly. "I just had three glasses of Moet, I am not even buzzing yet," she replies. "Yes you are and you need to slow down." "Look, let me do me please."

The bartender brings back the shots and each one of them grabs one. Sinclair holds her glass up in the air to make a toast. Turning to Jana, being very smart about it, she says, "To Jana's first one night stand!" Sinclair and Christy laugh, but Jana doesn't find Sinclair's gesture funny at all. Instead, she rolls her eyes at them and takes her shot.

Noticing her aggressive drinking from across the bar, two guys start pointing at Jana, gesturing for her to come over to sit with them. Christy notices the two men trying to get Jana's attention and signals back to them as to say that she was not coming over there. Seeing what Christy is doing, Jana reacts angrily. "Didn't I tell you to stay out of my business tonight?" she yells. "I am only trying to look out for you," Christy objects.

"Yeah Jana, you need to slow your role," adds Sinclair. "Look, just because you don't have a man Christy and your man Kenneth is a dog in here with another bitch, don't mean y'all can stop me from doing what the hell I want to do!" she says. "What you need to do, Sinclair, is go over there and handle your man and not try and handle me." "We are only trying to help, but since you want to be stubborn, you are on your own tonight." Sinclair responds. "Thank you!" Jana says.

Jana drains another glass of Moet, nearly stumbling from her seat. "Oops, y'all didn't see that," she says with a laugh. She heads to the other side of the bar, towards the two guys that sent the Moet to them. As she gets closer to her new 'friends', the guy's eyes light up when they notice what she is wearing. "Damn!" one of the guys says, as he sees the tightly fitted black skirt. Jana's skirt is so tight that if she bends over, you can easily see what she is wearing beneath that skirt. Barely keeping her balance, as she is walking in her black heels, she makes her way to an empty seat that the guys have saved for her.

"Hello gorgeous," one of the guys says to her. "How are you doing tonight? By the way, you are looking all so fine tonight." "Thank you," she says, turning to the other guy to indicate that she is choosing one of them in particular. "What is your name?" she asks the quiet guy. "James," he replies. "And you are?" he asks back. "My name is Jana." "Where are you from?" she asks. James responds that he is from LA, born and raised, and went that he attended UCLA on a football scholarship and now plays for the Washington Redskins.

"Wow," Jana jokes. "I just asked where you were from! I mean, do you always tell your life story when you first meet someone?" she says, laughing out loud. The other guy laughs hearing Jana's remarks. "Ok, now, why are you laughing along with me? What is your name? Mind you, I don't want to hear your life story!" she turns to him. "Well, excuse me, but my name is Chris." "Ok Chris, I wasn't talking to you so stay out of our business."

James and Chris look at each other, noting that Jana is clearly over the limit. They each have that devious look in their eyes that says that they are plotting something on her. Jana notices the looks they are exchanging. "What are y'all whispering?" "It's an inside thing," James responds. "Yes we want to get inside you," Chris says being very funny about what he just said. Jana, being rather drunk, does not really understand what Chris had said, and asks him to repeat it. "What did you just say?" "I was just talking to myself."

"Hmmm, whatever," she says. "I need to go to the restroom, so whatever you guys need to talk about you may proceed while I'm gone." "Are you coming back?" asks James. "Do you want me to come back?" "Why? Of course, the night is still young and I want to get to know you." "I bet you do."

As Jana leaves for the bathroom, the guys start their plotting. "Man, that bitch is fine as hell," Chris says. "I know." "Let's continue to get her ass drunk and take her back to the hotel, man." "I don't know about that, man," James says. "Her girls are going to put salt on our game. They are not going to let their girl leave with us," he adds. "We need a decoy. Let's see if we can get Reggie and Robert to occupy her girls while we handle the old girl. By the way, what was that bitch's name again?" "Shit, if I remember," James replies, laughing.

Sinclair and Christy, meanwhile, are still sitting at the bar and are watching the guys carefully while Jana is in the bathroom. They note all the giggles and reactions that James and Chris are making. Christy has a feeling that something was up. The guys notice that they were being watched and smile at Sinclair and Christy. Christy angrily shoots a bird back at them. James and Chris laugh, with a confused look on their faces, as if wondering what is going on. "We need to go check on her," says Sinclair. "I think she went to the bathroom," says Christy. "Let's go."

On the way to the bathroom to check on Jana, Sinclair is spotted by Precious, who whispers something into Kenneth's ear as he turns around and sees Sinclair. "What the fuck!" he says to himself. "How in the hell did she know that I was here?" he asks Precious. The girl he came with notices Kenneth's reactions and confronts him. "Do you know that girl?" "Yes I do." "Who is she?' "She is a close friend of mine." Precious finally tells Kenneth that she saw Sinclair in Shay's Salon earlier today but had forgotten to tell him.

"How can you forget to tell me that shit!" he yells at Precious. "Nigga, I fucking forgot, that's how!" She shouts back. "Stupid," he retorts angrily. "Don't get mad at me because you can't control your bitch. I'm not your fucking private investigator." "Whatever. Let me go over here and see what's up with her."

As he starts walking towards Sinclair and Christy, he notices several guys trying to get Sinclair's attention. He starts to get really jealous and begins to pick up his pace towards them, with a pool stick in one hand and a Corona in the other. As Christy notices Kenneth approaching them, she taps Sinclair on her back to warn her. She ignores Christy and proceeds to talk to one of the guys that stopped her.

"What's up Sinclair?" Kenneth greets her, but she proceeds to ignore him. "What, you can't hear me now?" Finally, she turns and faces him. "Don't you see that I'm talking to somebody?" Kenneth looks at the other guy. "No disrespect bro, but this is my girl." "Seems to me that she doesn't want to be bothered by you, man," the guy replies. "I'm going to bother your ass if you don't back the hell away from my girl," Kenneth says in an angry threatening voice.

In the mix of the back-forth trash talking, Sinclair interrupts Kenneth. "Oh, now I'm your girl! Was I your girl when you were lying about being with your agent when I clearly saw you with that light-skinned girl earlier today?" "What light skinned girl?" "That bitch who standing over their next to Precious." Kenneth looks in the direction of Precious.

"Damn dog, you are a real player," the guy says to Kenneth. "Shut the fuck up man and stay out of my business." "Come shut me up nigga!" "Stop it, stop it," screams Sinclair. "Look, I will talk to you later gorgeous," the guy tells Sinclair, as he begins to walk off. "Hey, what is your name?" Sinclair asks before he leaves. "Derrick," he replies. "Why do you want to know his name?" says Kenneth. "It's not as if you are going to talk to him again." "You are not my daddy and damn sure not my man," she replies, as she joins Christy on the way to the bathroom to check on Jana.

Realizing that he may have to change his approach to get Sinclair's attention, Kenneth heads back over to his pool table to finish his game. "So what happened?" Precious asks. "She's trying to play all hard and shit because she's with her friends." "Look, don't worry about her ass. You have me and my friend Natalia with you tonight." "What do you mean I have you and Natalia tonight?" he questions. "Do you know her?" "Yes," she says. He stares at them both. "Damn this is a small world."

"Why didn't you tell me that you two knew each other?" he asks Natalia, the girl he is with. "I didn't think that it was such a big deal. Plus, my girl told me what you were working with," Natalia replies with a laugh.

Although Kenneth has been Sinclair's man since high school, he still had a reputation about him—some good and some bad. Kenneth was known for his great basketball skills and it didn't hurt that he was going to be a first round selection in the upcoming NBA Draft. When girls heard about that, they flocked to him as if he was a gold mine. Natalia was no different from the rest. "Yes, so don't worry; if your girl does not act right, I will make sure that you're satisfied later tonight," says Natalia. Kenneth shakes his head and proceeds onto play pool.

As the girls enter the restroom to check on Jana, they hear a gagging sound coming from one of the stalls. "Jana," they call her name. "Are you ok?" Christy asks. Barley able to talk, she reassures them that she will be ok.

"I told you to slow down and that you were having too much to drink," says Sinclair. "Ok, maybe I just drank them to fast, but I will be just fine," Jana replies. "So what's up with those two guys you were talking to at the bar?" ask Sinclair. "You mean James and Chris." "Whatever their names are, but yes." "They are so cool; I mean I'm really feeling that James guy. Girls, he plays for the Washington Redskins." "Ok what else do you know about him besides that?" asks Christy.

"Well we really didn't have much time for a real conversation as of yet, but I will get all of that when I go back over there." "Wait a minute Jana, are you really going back over there?" say Sinclair. "Yes, why not?" "Because we think they are up to something and you need to be very careful." "I told y'all before that I am a big girl and I can take care of myself. Plus, I don't think I will be having anymore drinks tonight."

"Why don't you come over there with me Sinclair? I need someone to occupy Chris while I get to know James," she says with a smile. "I'm pretty sure Kenneth won't mind. By the way, have you talked to him yet?" "Yes, for a brief moment on my way here. He saw me talking to Derrick." "Derrick who?" Jana asks. "Oh, he is this guy that I just met on our way to check on you." "How does he look? Was he a football player?" "Girl I didn't ask all that and I don't care either," Sinclair responds. "Anyway, Kenneth saw me talking to him and damn near had a fit, girl." "That's what his ass gets," says Jana. "Did you ask him about the girl you saw him with?" "No. I wanted to see if he was going to tell me."

"Anyway, since you are ok, let's get back to our seats," Christy chips into their conversation. "And remember Jana, please be careful." "I promise I will," she replies.

As the girls exit the restroom and head back to the bar, they notice that the Pool Hall has gotten overly crowded. People start shouting out their sets, screaming their respected fraternity and sorority calls. The crowd is getting very intense and it does not help any that the DJ is playing the song "Where you from" by Master P. Trying to get back to their seats, the girls are pushed and bumped in the crowd. Suddenly, Sinclair notices Derrick, who pretty much saves her from the craziness that is going on.

Christy and Jana proceed on to their seats, while Sinclair and Derrick go to the dance floor. Although Derrick is trying to talk to her, she cannot hear a word that is coming from his mouth. They walk to a nearby corner of the Pool Hall that seems a little more pleasant for conversation. "I was waiting for you to come back," says Derrick. "Why is that?" "I wanted the opportunity to talk to you being that you are looking so beautiful tonight," he adds, looking into her eyes.

"So was that your boyfriend?" he asks, referring back to Kenneth. "Who?" she asks, pretending that she did not understand. "I like that, but you know who—the boy that was tripping earlier." "He was my boyfriend, but not anymore." "So, I guess, we can get to know each other then?" "Maybe," she replies. "Maybe," he responds with a smile. "Yes, maybe," she repeats with a blush.

"Wait, I forgot. I am moving to Atlanta in a month or two," she tells him. "Atlanta, why are you moving?" "I am from here and have lived in Baltimore my entire life. I think that it's time for a change," she replies. "I can respect that. I have something to tell you," he adds. "What?" "I'm going to be living in Atlanta as well." "Are you serious? How come?"

"I've just been traded to the Atlanta Falcons." "Oh so you are a football player?" Sinclair asks, disappointment in her voice. "Yes. But why do you say it like that?" "Because I think I had enough of the athletes. I think that y'all are nothing but dogs. My boyfriend, I mean my ex-boyfriend, plays basketball, and he is a big ass liar. I just don't trust y'all." "Well you can trust me. Look, how about we exchange numbers and we can talk about this later? We can go sit at the bar and have a drink and enjoy the rest of the night." "Sounds great," Sinclair replies.

Sinclair and Derrick exchange numbers. He gives her a hug and a kiss on the cheek, grabs her hand and navigates through the hectic crowd. On her way back to her seat, Sinclair sees Christy engaging into conversation with some guy. Derrick recognizes the guy Christy is talking to and calls his name. "Big Mike, what's up homeboy?" "Damn dog, I didn't know that you were in here," Mike replies. "What do you mean 'you didn't know'? This is my party that I am throwing." "I heard about your trade and shit," he says to Derrick. "That's why I am throwing this party. It's sort of a going away party for me."

"I see that my friend Jana has made her way back over to James and Chris," Sinclair says, pointing towards the trio still sitting at the bar. Mike looks over and notes that he knows James but remembers Chris through one of his homeboys. "Your girl needs to be careful with that old boy." "Which one?" Sinclair asks, rather concerned. "Chris," he says. "Why does she need to be careful?" "I heard that dude was spiking drinks and shit. He got in a trouble about that shit one time before. He also goes around telling people that he plays football and shit," says Mike. "So that nigga be lying?" says Derrick.

"We tried to tell her to be careful, but she would not listen. Anyway, I think that she is more interested in James," says Sinclair. "Good, cause she doesn't need to be fucking with that nigga Chris," says Mike.

As midnight approaches, the music is still playing, but the crowd on the dance floor is slowly decreasing. Sinclair, Derrick, Christy and Mike are enjoying each other's company, although the girls are still paying close attention to Jana across the bar. As the night progresses, the people start to focus more on the pool table area. You can hear the rumbling and the cursing in the back of the room. As the pool balls collide, the gambling scene is now on. Money is placed on all sides of the pool table.

Although very upset with him, Sinclair can't help but notice Kenneth betting as he is playing pool. Knowing that he may be drunk, she tries to ignore the fact that he is with people he should not to be around.

"What's wrong?" Christy asks, noticing her glances towards the pool area. "He is such an asshole. Look at him over there! He never gambles. I bet that his ass is drunk as hell," Sinclair says, anger evident in her voice. "Why are you so concerned about Kenneth?" "I'm not going to pretend that I don't care about his wellbeing." "Look Sinclair, just as Jana is an adult, so is Kenneth. And plus he is going to do what he wants to do anyway," says Christy. "A man is going to be a man. Let's just forget about him and enjoy each other's company," Derrick says with a smile.

It's now 2 o'clock and the crowd is moving from the Pool Hall onto the streets. Still, many people are inside, playing pool. One of those people is Kenneth. Derrick tells Sinclair that he needs to go to the bathroom and asks if she'd wait on his return. Sinclair happily agrees.

As Derrick heads to the bathroom, the girls prepare to leave flagging down Jana, indicating that she needs to come with them. Mike pays tab and just before he can sign the receipt, a loud explosion is heard from the pool table area. The girls and Mike look up to see Kenneth and Derrick fighting.

"What the hell?" yells Sinclair. "That's your boy and my man D going at it," says Mike. Punch for punch the two are going toe to toe. You can hear their shouts as they are fighting. "Punk ass nigga, I told you to leave my girl alone!" shouts Kenneth, as he continues to land some pretty good shots on Derrick. Bigger and much stronger, Derrick lifts Kenneth into the air and slams him onto the pool table.

The pool table breaks as Kenneth hits the ground. Soon, another fight breaks out. Pool balls and pool sticks start flying everywhere. Sinclair tries to make her way over to break the fight up. "I need to get Kenneth," she shouts. "Mike, try to get Derrick! We don't need this shit right now."

"They don't need to be getting into trouble over some dumb shit. They have their entire future ahead of them."

"Break it up man," Mike says to Derrick. "Kenneth, stop!" Sinclair screams. As Mike tries to break the fight up, Derrick is hit with a pool ball in the center of his knee. After the fight is finally over, Kenneth and Derrick walk towards the exit of the Pool Hall. "I think I messed up my fucking knee," Derrick shouts. Christy realizes that she too was hit by a flying pool stick. She has a small cut above her right eye.

"You are bleeding Christy," says Sinclair. "Where from?" she asks, clearly worried. "Above your right eye." "Damn, girl, it's time to go," Christy says with her hand over her right eye. Sinclair approaches Kenneth because she is concerned about his condition. "Are you ok?" "I'm good," he responds. "You need to get out of here before the police arrive. I am sure that they are on their way already," she tells him.

All Kenneth can think about is Derrick and the fact that all this started because she was entertaining him. "Are you going to talk to him?" "This is no time to be worrying about shit like that now. All you need to know is what I told you, and that was if you fuck up again I was done with your ass," she says. "You were with who you wanted to be with today because I saw her get out of your car." "Who, Natalia?" "I don't know what her name is and I don't really care!" "She is just a friend." "Well friends don't kiss friends in the mouth, and don't deny it, because I saw it with my own eyes."

Kenneth is confused, not knowing what Sinclair is talking about. Still, he cannot deny the fact that she is telling the truth. Kenneth is helped to his car and he asks Sinclair to meet him at the Waffle House on Mableton Drive. She agrees.

Christy is standing by Sinclair's car holding a napkin to her face.

"How is your face?" Sinclair asks. "I will be ok." "It's not such a huge cut." The girls get inside the car and notice that Jana is nowhere to be found. "Damn," says Christy. "Where could she be?" "We can't leave her, we have to find her." As the girls look around the strip area, they spot James. "James!" they shout. James walks to their car. "What's up?"

"Where is Jana?" "She might be with Chris." "Why would she leave with Chris?" "All I know is that he invited her to come with him to an after hour party. When the fight broke out, I was trying to get out of there; I can't be getting into any trouble and shit." "Where is the after hour spot?" "He didn't say."

The girls drive off down the strip, calling Jana's cell phone, but there's no answer. They leave numerous voicemails and continue to repeatedly call her cell phone, but to no avail, as there is no answer from Jana. "We can't leave her with somebody she doesn't even know," Sinclair says. "Let's just pray that she is ok." With all this drama that just happened in the Pool Hall, the girls struggle to hold their emotions back.

Chris and Jana are on their way to D.C. He notices that Jana is fading in as she had too much to drink. He gives her what she thinks is a Tylenol and a bottle of water. What he was really giving her was a date rape pill. Jana takes the pill and soon passes out.

He looks at her body with a smile on his face. "Are you awake?" he asks. There is no response from Jana. Chris is actually from the D.C. area and owns a couple of rental properties. He has used one of his rental properties before to assault a victim in the past. Once there, he pulls up into the garage, gets out, goes over to the passenger side of the car and carries Jana into the house. Jana barely stirs as he lays her on the bed.

"Where are we?" she asks as she comes around. "We are at my place." "Why are we here?" "Because I want you all to myself," he responds, taking off his shirt and then his pants. He gets on the bed with Jana and starts taking off her dress. "What are you doing?" "Just relax, I'm going to give you what you need," He tries to calm her down. She tries to fight him off but is too weak to do so.

Chris strips her down to her panties, looks at her almost naked body, and then takes them off. Jana is trembling, as she watches Chris remove his boxers. He climbs on top of her and forces his penis inside of her. Jana cries out in pain and yells for him to stop but Chris continues his penetration until he comes inside of her.

With no knowledge of where Jana is, Sinclair and Christy head to the Waffle House to meet up with Kenneth. On the way, she gets a call from Derrick. "Hello," she answers. "I want to apologize for what happened tonight," he says. "What the hell happened between you and Kenneth?" "I was heading to the bathroom and your boy came out of nowhere and hit me in the back of my head." "I had to protect myself you know. I can't be letting know punk run up on me for nothing."

"Both of y'all were acting really childishly." "Well, I said what I had to say and I hope that this doesn't interfere with our friendship." "It won't Derrick, trust me. I have to talk to you later because Jana is somewhere with this dude Chris." "What is she doing with him?" "I don't know, but we have to find her fast." "All I know is that the nigga lives in D.C.," says Derrick. "D.C.!" yells Sinclair. "Shit, I have to go, because I need to find her." "Ok talk to you later," he responds and hangs up.

Sinclair tries to reach Jana one more time, but as soon as she begins to dial the number, she sees a car pull up beside Kenneth's and some guy starts yelling at him through the window. "What's up nigga? " the guy yells. "You lost on the pool table and I want my money," He adds, referring to the fact that, earlier tonight Kenneth lost $1000 to the guy. "I'm going to pay you your money nigga, so fuck you," Kenneth retorts. After Kenneth says that, gunshots are fired into his SUV and the car drives off. Sinclair and Christy run up to his car and see Kenneth bent over the steering wheel, apparently dead.

CHAPTER 3

It is 6:37 am on Sunday morning, and Sinclair and Christy are still shocked at what just happened hours earlier. Sinclair's eyes are pouring with tears as Christy tries to comfort her. "How could this be happening?" Sinclair says. "How could a night of celebration turn to tragedy so quickly? I feel as if it's my fault," she adds. "You can't blame this on yourself," Christy tries to reassure her. "Things happen for a reason and you should just leave it in God's hands."

Despite trying to calm down, Sinclair is still unable to hold back her tears. Grandma hears the weeping coming from Sinclair's room. She knocks on the door, and enters with the Bible in her hand. "Baby, I know the pain you are feeling inside, but everything is going to be ok. You need to be strong and pray to the Lord to pull you through this tragedy."

Sinclair is sitting on the side of her bed with her face buried in her hands, as Grandma tries to comfort her with words of wisdom. "Christy, go downstairs and fix her a glass of orange juice," says Grandma. "Yes ma'm," Christy replies and walks out of the room. Grandma sits beside Sinclair on her bed and puts her arm around her. She brings Sinclair's head into her chest and tells her to let those tears out. "Let it out baby; you will feel much better if you can just let it all out." As Grandma holds her, Sinclair's sobs start getting louder and louder. "Why did this have to happen, why?" "I don't know baby," says Grandma. "All I know is that he's in a better place now so don't you worry about a thing."

After a while, Grandma finally gets Sinclair to calm down a bit. Christy comes back with the orange juice that Grandma asked her to get. "Here baby drink this, it will make you feel better." She drinks some of the orange juice and puts the rest on the nightstand next to the bed. Grandma hands the bible to her and tells her to read David's Song of Praise. She turns to Samuel 22: 3-7 and reads the following prayer.

"The Lord is my rock, my fortress, and my savior; my God is my rock, in who I find protection. He is my shield, the power that saves me, and my place of safety. He is my refuge, my savior, the one who saves me from violence. I called on the Lord, who is worthy of my praise, and he saved me from my enemies. The waves of death overwhelmed me; floods of destruction swept over me. The grave wrapped its ropes around me; death laid a trap in my path. But in my distress I cried out loud to the Lord; yes, I cried to my God for help. He heard me from his sanctuary; my cry reached his ears."

Sinclair closes the Bible after she reads it, looks into the sky and says to the Lord, "Thank you." Grandma comes back into the room and asks the girls to come to church with her. The girls agree. "I don't have anything to wear," Christy says to Sinclair. She smiles at Christy and tells her that she is welcome to wear something from her closet. Grandma tells Sinclair to wake her sister up and help her find something to wear to church. "Tiffany get up, we have to get ready for church," Sinclair urges her.

Grandma goes downstairs to prepare breakfast for everyone. Sinclair gathers Tiffany's clothes for church, while Christy looks for something to wear from her closet. "This is a beautiful blue dress," she says. "I think I will wear this one." Sinclair notices the dress that Christy picked out. "That's the dress that Kenneth brought for me to wear when we went to the Maxwell concert a few months ago." "Oh I'm sorry, I didn't know. I will put it back and find something else." "Oh no, it's not a problem; it just brings back some memories of what happened that night, that's all." "What happened?" Christy asks.

"After the concert, we went to The Hill and he surprised me with some strawberries and wine as we sat in the car watching the stars that night." "Wow, how romantic," says Christy. "And before you knew it, we were having this passionate kiss as if we had just met each other. I still remember his hands gently rubbing my body and my hands rubbing his body." Sinclair is in a daze with a big smile on her face as she pauses for a brief moment of reflection.

Christy snaps her fingers at Sinclair. "What else happened?" she asks, impatient to hear more. She continues to tell her story. "He unbuttons my dress and before you know, I am naked. He sits me in his lap and starts to caress my nipples with his soft lips. I remember looking into his eyes. He was looking at me as if I was a piece of meat that he had to have.

He gets a condom out and removes it from the package. He puts it on and, moments later, I am riding him like a horse." "Nasty," says Christy with a smile on her face. "Knowing all that, I think that I'd prefer to wear something else," she jokes.

They both laugh in response to what Christy just said. Tiffany enters Sinclair's room, dressed and ready for church. "I heard you crying," she says. "What happened?" "Kenneth got shot last night." "Is he dead?" "Yes, some guys he was arguing with last night shot him in his truck." "I'm sorry," says Tiffany. "I am going to miss him." "Me too," says Sinclair.

Grandma calls the girls downstairs for breakfast. Once again, the smell of bacon, eggs, grits, and toast is in the air. "That's a smell that I will never get tired of," says Sinclair. "I like that smell," says Tiffany. As the girls sit at the table for breakfast, in comes Uncle Pete. "Hello my beautiful ladies, how are y'all this morning?" "Fine," the girls respond.

Uncle Pete sits down at the head of the table. He stares at Sinclair, noticing her body language. "How are you holding up?" Before she answers, he asks another question. "Were you involved with any of this?" "That girl has been through a lot in short period of time, have some respect," Grandma interjects. "I'm just saying, Momma, I don't want my niece to be involved in any wrongdoings out there," he says.

"I didn't do anything to anybody," Sinclair says. "Yes we had our differences, but I certainly didn't have anything to do with his death. I can't believe you would say or think such a thing. You treat me as if I am a suspect, Uncle Pete!" she cries out. "May I be excused?" she asks Grandma. "Baby, eat your breakfast, and Pete leave that girl alone. If you continue to bother her with that foolishness, I am going to run your butt out of here. Did I make myself clear?"

"I am sorry," he says. "Don't tell me; Sinclair is the one that needs your apology." "I just want the best for you and I will do anything to protect you from any danger. I am sorry if I offended you," He says to Sinclair, who smiles and says that she forgives him. She adds that she is fully aware that he has her back and wants to keep her away from any danger. They put their differences aside and proceed to have breakfast in silence.

As they start getting ready to go to the 11 o'clock church service, Sinclair's cell phone rings and there is a knock at Grandma's front door. She answers her cell phone and Uncle Pete answers the door. The phone call is from Jana. "Jana, where are you?" "I am in D.C." Why are you in D.C.?" "Chris brought me here last night." "Why did you leave with him?"

"Chris was telling me about this after hour party that his boy was having and asked me to come with him." "How stupid can you be?" "I know. I have to tell you something," Jana says while crying. "Please, less drama, as I have already been through enough already," says Sinclair. "Chris raped me." "What?" "Yes, all I remember after getting into his car is lying in his bed naked and him on top of me. I tried to make him stop but he wouldn't." "Did you call the police?" asks Sinclair.

Before Jana can respond to Sinclair's question, Chris comes back into the room and Jana quickly tells her that she has to go and will call her back. "Wait," shouts Sinclair, but Jana has already hung up the phone. "That was Jana," Sinclair says to everyone. "What's wrong?" asks Christy. "She's with Chris and she said that he raped her." "Oh my God!" says Christy. "We have to find out where she is and go get her," Sinclair urges.

While the girls are trying to figure out what to do about Jana's situation, they notice Uncle Pete talking with two men at the front door. "Sinclair, the two detectives here want to speak with you," he says. Uncle Pete invites the two detectives in and asks them to have a seat. "Hello, I am Detective Williams and this is Detective Smith," one of the two men makes the introduction. "Hello," says Sinclair. "I was wondering if we could ask you some questions about the death of your friend last night." "What is it that you would like to know?" Sinclair asks, suddenly rather frightened.

She sits down in a chair across from the detectives with a puzzled look on her face. "It seems that the guys spotted in the shooting accident were friends of yours," says Detective Williams. "What do you mean by 'friends of mine'?" "We were told by two women that that the two men who killed your friend were talking with you at the Pool Hall earlier that night." "What two girls?" "Precious Brown and Natalia Lundy," he responds.

"The only guy I was talking to was Derrick and he had a friend with him named Mike. Are you saying that they were the ones that killed Kenneth?" "It's a possibility but we are not sure until we find out where they are." Sinclair sits back into her chair with a confused look on her face. "Is there anything you can tell us about that night?" asks Detective Smith.

Sinclair starts to explain what she saw that night at the Waffle House. "All I remember is getting a call from Kenneth to meet him there. When we arrived, we noticed a black Mercedes pull beside his car. I heard Kenneth and the other driver yelling at each other, after which several gun shots were fired." "Did you see the faces of the assailants?" "No, I didn't."

"Do you have a way to contact your friend Derrick?" "Yes, I have his cell phone number." "We need for you to call him and get some information from him." "What do you want me to say?" "Mainly we need to know what kind of car he has so we can at least make sure that the car matches the description of the one seen at the scene of the shooting."

Sinclair gets up to go in the kitchen to call Derrick. Meanwhile, Detective Smith talks to Christy to find out more information pertaining to last night's incident. "I remember that Derrick and Kenneth got in this huge fight over Sinclair. And as we were leaving the Pool Hall, Derrick was in a lot of pain, barley able to walk on his right leg. He kept saying that he probably messed up his knee from the fight and, if he couldn't play football because of the injury, he would kill Kenneth for ruining his career. He sounded so serious when he was saying that." The detective takes Christy's statement and waits patiently for Sinclair to return.

Sinclair is now on the phone with Derrick in the kitchen. "Hello," says Derrick. "How are you?" "Not so god," she responds. "Much had happened in such a short period of time. Kenneth was shot and killed last night." "Are you serious?" "We have no idea who could have done such a thing." "I feel sorry for your loss. Is there anything that I can do for you?" "No, not really."

"How is your leg?" "It feels a little better than last night. I think I will be ok to play football this season. I went to see the trainer this morning and they did an X-ray on my knee and said that I had a sprained knee." "I am so sorry to hear that. Still, you will recover, but Kenneth's life is over. He is gone for good."

Seemingly oblivious that she is upset about Kenneth's death, all Derrick is talking about is his knee and the fact that he thought that he wasn't going to play football this upcoming season. "Can you get over yourself? Your knee will be fine." "I don't know why your punk ass boyfriend attacked me last night. He was lucky that I didn't kill him myself in the Pool Hall last night." "Why would you say something like that knowing the he is actually dead?" "I'm sorry; I'm just disappointed it went down like that last night." After exchanging some harsh words, they calm down a bit and Sinclair uses the opportunity to ask him the question that the detective needs.

"Were you able to drive home last night?" "Yes, I drove home, even though I was in pain. You know I can't let anybody drive my Benz," "Oh you have a Benz. It must be nice. It's better than my silver Honda Accord." "Your silver can't touch that black Benz of mine." "Oh my God," she screams. "What?" "Never mind, we are getting ready to go to church so I have to go." She hangs up the phone and starts pacing back and forth in the kitchen.

Grandma comes in the kitchen to check on her. "What did you find out?" "I think Derrick had something to do with Kenneth's death. He was very upset after they got into that fight because of his injured knee. He kept saying last night that he could have killed Kenneth in the Pool Hall." "Are you sure that he had something to do with it?" "I'm sure." "How sure are you? Please consider this carefully, as these are serious charges."

"On the night of the shooting, the car that was beside Kenneth's SUV was a black Mercedes Benz, Grandma. In addition, Precious recognized Derrick and his friends as well, because police officers have it in their statement she gave them. Grandma, he was the only guy I was talking to last night." "You have to go in there and tell the detectives what you told me." "Yes ma'm."

Sinclair and Grandma leave the kitchen join the detectives in the living room. As she sits down, tears start pouring from her eyes. "It was Derrick." "Are you sure?" asks Detective Williams. "Yes, because he told me what kind of car he was driving that night and it was a black Mercedes Benz that Precious witnessed at the crime scene." "In that case, we have to get a warrant for his arrest."

"Can you give us his last name?" "Yes it's Spaulding; Derrick Spaulding." "What about his friend's name?" "Mike

Davis," Christy joins in. "Thank you, ladies, for your cooperation on this investigation; if we have any more questions, we will reach out to you. In the meantime, if you have any questions for us, here is my card; please don't hesitate to call." "Thank you," Uncle Pete says, as he escorts the detectives out of the house.

I can't believe Derrick and Mike would do such a thing," says Christy. "They seemed so nice when we were talking to them," Sinclair agrees. "You can never judge a book by its cover. You never know what people's intentions are until you really get to know them or push someone to the edge. Now, with all that said and done, let's go to the church and ask God for forgiveness and to pray over your friends' wounded souls," Grandma suggests. With that, they all gather their things and leave the house to attend the 11 o'clock church service.

The family pulls up into Hopewell Baptist Church. A huge crowd is expected, being that it is the first Sunday of the month. On their way inside the church, Sinclair sees Kenneth's mother, Kathryn. Tears begin to fill her eyes, as she has no idea what to say to the grief-stricken woman. "What do I say Grandma?" "Just say what's in your heart."

Sinclair continues walking towards Mrs. Kathryn, tears still running down her cheeks. She gets Kathryn's attention and hugs her very tightly. Mrs. Kathryn puts her arms around her and gives her a hug. "It's going to be ok. We are all felling the hurt and pain of his death, but we need to be strong," she tells her in a low voice. Sinclair explains to Kathryn that she and Kenneth were having an argument earlier on the day of his death and that she feels responsible for his death.

"It's my fault; I didn't want anything to do with him that day and because of that he is dead." "Look, it's not your fault, so stop blaming yourself. I know how you feel about Kenneth despite y'all disagreement." "I really loved him." "I know baby, I know." After a few minutes of sharing their grief, Sinclair looks into Kathryn's eyes and begins to tell her about last night.

"They have a suspect in the murder of your son's death," says Sinclair. "Thank God. Who is it?" "A guy named Derrick who Kenneth got into a fight with. They have a warrant for his arrest."

During the service, the pastor talks about the loss of one their congregation. He talks about Kenneth and all the positive things that he could remember about him since he was a little kid. He also talks about the love for the enemies, in reference to Kenneth's suspects. The pastor notes:

"You have heard the law says, 'love your neighbor' and hate your enemy. But I say, love your enemies! Pray for those who persecute you! In that way, you will be acting as true children of your Father in heaven. For he gives his sunlight to both the evil and the good and he sends rain on the just and the unjust alike. If you love only those that love you, what reward is there for that? Even corrupt tax collectors do that much. If you are kind only to your friends, how are you different from anyone else? Even pagans do that. But you are to be perfect, even as your father in heaven is perfect. Mathew 5: 43-48

As the service comes to a close, the pastor acknowledges Mrs. Kathryn and sends his prayers out to her. The church takes up a collection for her son's funeral arrangements. Mrs. Kathryn thanks all the members with a smile of joy. Although hurt inside, she hides her emotions well. Sinclair approaches her again. "When will the funeral take place?" "Next Saturday," she replies. Sinclair gives her a final hug for the day and they all leave the church.

"It was very nice of them to take up a collection for Kenneth's funeral arrangements," says Grandma. "That boy had so much God-given talent. I think he was going to be a first round selection in this year NBA Draft," Uncle Pete adds. "Can we please not talk about Kenneth right now?" Sinclair asks, unable to bear any more pain. "Ok baby." "Oh my God," Sinclair suddenly shouts. "What is it?" Christy asks. "I have calls and messages from Jana and some other numbers. Let me check them and see what is going on.

When she dials into her cell phone to check her messages, she learns that Jana had left urgent messages telling her that she is in D.C. and needs for them to come pick her up as soon as possible. Along with Jana's messages, Sinclair hears a message from Detective Williams, saying that they have Derrick Spaulding in custody. The final message is from Derrick, saying that they have him as a suspect for Kenneth's murder, asking her to come to the police station.

After hearing all the messages, she hangs up the phone. "Who were the messages from?" asks Christy. "They were from Jana, Detective Williams and Derrick. They have him in custody and Jana needs us to come get her." "Well let's call Jana, so we can go get her."

They arrive back at home to change clothes. In their haste to get to Jana, they are rushing, nearly knocking over everything they pass. "Do y'all want me to come just in case Chris is there?" Uncle Pete asks. "No," they respond. After they change, they rush back downstairs out the front door to Sinclair's car. "Wait," Christy urges suddenly. "Let's call Jana and get the directions before we leave."

She dials the number and Jana answers. "Where exactly are you?" "I am standing outside in this sub division called Legacy Walk." "Do you have an address?" "No. Wait, I see someone standing outside. I will ask." She walks to a man standing outside. "Excuse me sir, can you give me the address to where I am?" The man gives her the address and Jana quickly passes it on to Sinclair. "Please hurry and come get me."

On the way to Jana, Sinclair gets a call from Detective Williams, who starts telling her that they have Derrick but they don't have Mike. "Derrick claims his innocence and is just repeating that he didn't have anything to do with Kenneth's murder." She tells the detective that he called and left her a message to come see him at the station. "I am on my way to get my friend from D.C. and, as soon as I get back, I will come to the station," she adds.

Once they arrive in D.C., they begin to ask several pass-ersby for the exact location to the sub division. After a few minutes of riding around, they finally locate the address Jana has given them. Soon, Sinclair spots Jana standing on the sidewalk. They pull up, jump out of the car and run to Jana with open arms. Jana is overwhelmed with joy to see her friends again.

"I am so glad to see y'all." "How are you feeling?" asks Christy, concern evident in her voice. "I feel so badly about what happened last night; how could I be so stupid?" she cries out. "We know you, Jana, and it wasn't your fault," Sinclair tries to reassure her. Once she says that, Jana starts to shed tears. "I should have never put myself in that situation. I should have just listened to y'all and been more careful."

"We all make mistakes, and all we can do is learn from them," says Christy. "Where is Chris?" asks Sinclair. "He left this morning and told me to find my way back." "That bastard!" shouts Christy. "I didn't trust his ass when I looked at him from across the bar," she adds. "He just looked sneaky as hell." "What we need to do is get you back home and to the emergency room to get checked out," suggests Sinclair. "We are definitely pressing charges on his ass today," she adds. The girls jump back into the car and leave for home.

As the girls are leaving D.C., Sinclair tells Jana what happened last night after they left the Pool Hall. "Kenneth is dead." "Are you serious?" "He was shot in the parking lot of the Waffle House last night." "How are you holding up?" "I'm still hurt, but I feel a little better that the police have some-one in custody for his death." "Who was it that shot him?" "I met this guy Derrick last night..." Before Sinclair could finish her sentence, Jana interrupts her, "The guy that was fighting with Kenneth?" "Yes," she responds.

"We think Derrick had something to do with Kenneth be-ing shot. When I pulled up to the Waffle House to meet up with Kenneth, I saw a black Mercedes Benz that Derrick owns. It was next to Kenneth's car and the guys shot Kenneth from inside it." As she continues to explain what happened, she mentioned that she saw James at the time they were looking for her and that James didn't know where she was.

Jana looked confused. "Wait a minute," she said. "James and Chris were together when we left Palace Place. Before we ever left Chris, I pulled around the back of the Pool Hall to wait for James. That's when we started having drinks and, before I knew it, I was lying on the back seat of Chris's car. I must have passed out, as after that, I don't know what happened. What I do know is that James drives a black Mercedes Benz as well."

"How do you know that James has a black Benz?" Sinclair asks. "Girl you know me, that's one of the first things I ask guys when I meet them," she replies. "While we were inside the Pool Hall, Chris kept saying that he had to take care of some business. He was talking about some nigga that owes him 1,000 dollars and if that nigga don't pay he was going to kill his ass that night."

"Precious told the police that the guys that shot Kenneth were guys that we were talking to at the Pool Hall," Sinclair explains. "I saw Precious as I was leaving the Pool Hall, so she probably grouped all of us together, not being specific to the police." "I have a bad feeling about the turnout of this," says Christy. "I think the detectives have the wrong guy," she adds. "I can't believe that James would sit there and lie to my face about not knowing where you were," say Sinclair.

"Now that I think about it, I could have been in the back seat of James's car when and if they killed Kenneth." "We have to hurry back and get to the police station, so that we can explain what you just told us," urges Sinclair. "I am also going to report rape on that nigga Chris," Jana agrees, her voice full of anger. The girls are back on the freeway en route to Baltimore when Sinclair gets a call from Grandma. "I'm calling to see if y'all got Jana." "Yes Grandma, we got her." Sinclair explains to Grandma what Jana revealed to them and promises that they will be home soon.

They finally arrive back in Baltimore. As soon as Sinclair pulls into the police station and parks, they all jump out and enter through the door. "We need to see Detective Williams or Detective Smith," Sinclair explains to the deputy officer at the reception desk. "Have a seat and I get him for you," replies the deputy. About five minutes later, Detective Williams comes to the front.

"Hello Sinclair." Nervously and anxiously, Sinclair begins to tell Detective Williams what Jana told her. "You have the wrong man," she says. "Jana, tell the detective what you told me." Jana begins to tell the detective everything she could remember about that night. She even tells him that the car that was seen at the crime belonged to James and that James and Chris were the real shooters.

"Are you sure?" says Detective Williams. "I'm sure," says Jana. "Describe this Chris to me." Jana begins to describe Chris's appearance and the deputy makes a sketch of every detail that Jana is giving them. "He's about 6'2 and about 210 lbs, has brown skin, and a low haircut. Oh yeah, he has a tattoo on his forearm that looks like hands that are praying."

With the sketch that they have, the deputy also gives them a line-up book to see if they can recognize anybody in there. As they are looking through the book, they indeed notice Chris's photo and point this out to the detective. The detective looks at the picture and inputs his information in the computer. "It looks like we've already had a warrant for his arrest."

"So what about Derrick?" asks Sinclair. "Well, we still have to book him, and, according to the standard procedure in a murder case, being that he is still a suspect, we have to set bail for him." "But he didn't do it," objects Sinclair. "That may be true, but until we do a full investigation on the case, we have to assume that he is involved." "Well, can I at least see him?" "Sure."

Before the detective heads to the back to get Derrick, Jana mentions that she was raped by Chris and that she wants to press charges. She explains to him what took place that night. "He drugged me and took me all the way to D.C. and raped me." The detective takes her statement and tells her that they would charge Chris with kidnapping and felony rape.

Sinclair is waiting patiently to see Derrick. "I feel so stupid," she says. "I should have not made any assumptions until I had all the facts." Finally, she is called to the back of the station to see Derrick. As precautionary measures, Derrick is brought out in handcuffs and shackles. He is suited up in an orange jump suit, as if they had already found him guilty. "What the hell is going on?" he yells as soon as he sees Sinclair. "We are going to get you out of here," Sinclair responds. "I told them about how upset you were and that your car matched the car that was at the scene of the crime. I'm sorry," she says. After hearing that, Derrick gets even more upset. "I can't believe that you would think that I would do something like that!" he yells and, without any hesitation, he gets up and leaves the room in anger.

CHAPTER 4

Once the girls leave the police station, they are on their way back to Grandma's home and Christy realizes that she left her car parked at Park Place. "Damn, with all the things that have been going on, I forgot my car." Sinclair turns around and takes Christy there to pick up her car. "Jana, how do you feel?" asks Sinclair. "I feel ok. I will be fine."

"I'm just glad that Chris is going to pay the price for what he did." The girls all agree as they continue their journey to Christy's car. "Hey Sinclair, what did Derrick say to you when you saw him?" Christy asks. "I tried to explain to him what happened. Girl, he was so upset that he didn't want to hear anything I had to say. I feel so badly because of the pain and humiliation I put him through."

"Everything will be ok," Jana tries to reassure her. As they approach Christy's car, Jana gets a phone call. She reaches in her purse to retrieve her phone, looks to see who is calling her and recognizes James's number. "What the fuck?" she yells. Sinclair and Christy notice the shocked expression on her face. "What's wrong?" Sinclair asks. "It's James calling me." "Answer the phone and see what he has to say." The girls pull next to Christy's car as Jana answers the call. "Hello," she greets his hesitantly. "What happened to you last night?" he asks. Unable to control her emotions, she burst out, "You motherfucker!" "What's wrong and why are you yelling at me?" he asks.

"Whether you know it or not, your friend Chris raped me last night." "You are kidding me!" "Don't act as if you didn't know what happened to me. I wasn't that drunk to not remember you getting in the car with me and Chris last night." After Jana says that, there is a brief silence between the two. James stars to wonder if Jana really knows anything.

"What do you remember?" "I wasn't too drunk to remember Chris telling you that Kenneth owed him a thousand dollars. I also know that you drive a black Mercedes Benz." "What are you trying to say?" "On the night of the shooting, the witnesses reported seeing the suspects in a black Mercedes Benz like yours. It all seems to add up now. With the rape and the Kenneth's murder, you and Chris are going to jail."

As Jana hangs up the phone, her eyes well up with tears. "He acts as if he doesn't know what happened last night. I hope they catch the both of them and throw them in the jail." The girls continue to sit in the Sinclair's car for a few more minutes, trying to figure out what to do in the meantime. "If James or Chris tries to contact you, do not answer anymore of their calls," Sinclair advises.

"You need to have as little contact with them as possible, so that we can focus on positive things until this is over," she adds and Jana nods in agreement. After that Christy and Jana say goodbye, get into Christy's car and they leave Park Place.

In the meantime, James is still puzzled, worrying if Jana may be on to something. During the entire time that he was on the phone with her, Chris was sitting next to him. "I think that she knows a little too much about last night," he says. "She told me that she heard you saying that Kenneth owed you a thousand dollars. She also remembers me telling her that I drive a black Benz."

"So?" Chris questions. "So!" James yells back. "Why didn't you tell me that you fucked her last night?" Chris stares at James with a surprised look on his face. "She said that you raped her, man," he adds. "What does it matter if I did or not? The little freak got what she wanted." "Man, I can't get into any trouble for this shit!"

"You are not going to get into any trouble." "I'd better not, because if I do, I will tell the police everything that happened that night." "What we need to do is find the girls and I will take it from there," says Chris. "What do you have in mind?"

Not knowing that the girls have already gone to the police to report what happened, Chris and James try to come up with a scheme to get rid of the girls. "Remember, if they are the only witnesses and we get rid of them, then the police won't have any evidence that we were there on the night of the shooting," says Chris. "What about my car?" James asks. "You are not the only person that has a black Benz. In the meantime, we lay low."

Back at home, Sinclair is approached by Grandma and Uncle Pete. Grandma gives her a hug. "Is everything alright with Jana?" Sinclair starts telling them about what happened to Jana and what she told them in the car. "My God," exclaims Grandma in shock. "That poor girl," Uncle Pete adds, clearly very upset. He shouts out, "That bastard!" referring to Chris. "Somebody needs to kill him for what he has done."

"Enough of that killing talk," says Grandma. "Violence is not the answer. Never wish that on anybody. God will take care of them." "Sometimes God waits too long," retorts Uncle Pete, as he leaves Grandma's house. "Where are you going Pete?" "Just to the front yard, to take a smoke." Grandma shakes her head with a smile and says, "What am I going to do with him?"

"I know what will make you feel better," She turns to Sinclair. "What?" Sinclair asks. "Grandma will make your favorite Sunday dinner and you can invite Christy and Jana over to join us." "That would be nice." "In the meantime, you need to go get relaxed by taking a nice bath and getting some rest until I finish supper." Sinclair thanks Grandma and hugs her telling her how much she loves her. She heads upstairs to prepare herself for the remainder of the evening. "That baby has been through so much, but God is going to work it out," says Grandma.

Tiffany enters Sinclair's room. "Are you still sad?" "Yes, I'm a little sad, but I will be ok. I am going to take a nice bath and get ready for Grandma's good cooking we will be enjoying later today. In the meantime, why don't you go help Grandma prepare the dinner?" "Ok," Tiffany replies. Sinclair goes into the bathroom to prepare her bath and Tiffany joins Grandma and Uncle Pete downstairs.

"I am here to help you Grandma," says Tiffany. "I can use all the help you can give me, baby." Meanwhile, Sinclair is upstairs looking in the mirror. Not having had much rest, she notices the bags under her eyes and the pallor of her skin. "I am looking sick right now." She stops her water from over running out of the tub, takes off her clothes and gets into her bubble bath she prepared.

"This feels so good," she says. "I can sit here all day." About ten minutes pass by and Sinclair falls asleep from the exhaustion. She begins to dream passionately about Kenneth.

The lights are dimmed and the candles are lit around the bathtub. There are strawberries and wine next to the bathtub as well. Soft music is playing in the background. Kenneth enters the bathroom, with just a towel wrapped around his waist, letting it drop onto the floor. Sinclair looks at him with a smile and invites him in to join her. He gets in the tub, his hands gently rubbing her legs; she brings him close to have a kiss. Kenneth leans in between her legs, and kisses her passionately. Sinclair says to him that she wants all of him inside of her. With her legs spread, Kenneth moves in between them, whispering how much he wants her. "Can I have you?" "Yes," she responds. He asks again. "Can I have you?" "Yes," she repeats passionately. Sinclair then repeats yes, yes, yes, out very loudly.

"Sinclair, telephone," Tiffany calls her from outside of the bathroom. After dozing off for nearly forty-five minutes in the tub, she realizes that she was having a dream about Kenneth. She is surprised by how real it felt. "Bring me the phone," she tells Tiffany. "Who is calling?" "It's Christy." She takes the phone. "Hey girl," says Christy. "What are you doing?" "I was taking a bath and started dreaming about Kenneth. It's going to take me a while to get over him." "I understand. I just got a call from Mike; you know the guy that was with Derrick at the Pool Hall, and he is on his way to bail him out of jail." "That's great," Sinclair responds. "Apparently, when he was talking to Derrick, he told him that he was sorry for the way he acted when you came to see him. He also went on to say that Derrick mentioned that he was very frustrated and that he didn't want his reputation to be ruined by this false accusation. But he does want to see you and he will call you when he gets out."

After hearing the good news, Sinclair's smile spread from cheek to cheek. "Thank you for calling me and telling me that, girl!" she exclaimed. Before they hung up the phone, she added, "I forgot to tell you that Grandma is inviting you and Jana over for dinner tonight." "Count me in," says Christy. "I will call Jana to let her know," says Sinclair. "See y'all later," she adds before hanging up.

Sinclair calls Jana to give her the news about Derrick and invite her to join them for dinner at her house. After that, she finally gets out of the tub and prepares for the evening. After getting dressed, she heads over to her bed. Noticing the pictures she threw into the corner of her room yesterday during the graduation celebration, she gathers them up from the floor and begins to organize them into a photo book.

As she sees the many pictures of her mom and some of other members of the family, she notices one in particular—that of her and Kenneth when they were about ten years old. She picks the photo up, smiling at the happy memories of them. "I can't believe that we've known each other for such a long time." As she continues to go through the shoebox full of photos, she sees many more photos of her and Kenneth from their high school days. Many are of Kenneth playing basketball. As tears begin to well up in her eyes, she quickly puts the photos next to her on the bed. She remembers what Grandma used to tell her about picking up the Bible and reading it when times get hard. Sinclair begins to read a scripture from John 14: 15-21.

> "If you love me, obey my commandments. And I will ask the Father, and he will give you another Advocate, who will never leave you. He is the Holy Spirit, who leads into all truth. The world cannot receive him, because it isn't looking for him and doesn't recognize him. But you know him, because he lives with you now and later will be you. No, I will not abandon you as orphans- I will come to you. Soon the world will no longer see me, but you will see me. Since I live, you also will live. When I am raised to life again, you will know that I am in my Father, and you are in me, and I am in you. Those who accept my commandments and obey them are the ones

who love me. And because they love me, my father will
love them. And I will love them and reveal myself to
each of them."

When she finished, she closes the Bible, holds it tightly into her chest and repeats, "Thank you God," three times before saying, "Amen." She puts the Bible next to her bed. Just as she starts getting comfortable, she grabs her cell phone to call Kenneth's mother Kathryn. She wants to know if there is anything that she can do to help with the funeral arrangements. "Hello Mrs. Kathryn, how are you?" "I'm making it," she responds in a tearful voice. "I was wondering if you needed me for anything related to your son's funeral arrangements for next Saturday."

"Maybe you could help me prepare the reception for after the funeral." "I would be more than happy to help you," says Sinclair. "I also have some god news about Kenneth's case," she adds. "What can be so good about my son's murder? No matter what, it want bring my son back." "I'm sorry. I didn't mean it like that," Sinclair apologizes for her inconsiderate outburst. "I know that you didn't, baby. What is it that you know about my son's case?"

Sinclair goes on to tell her about the new investigation that the detectives have from her friend Jana's statement. "That's great news," says Mrs. Kathryn. "I was so afraid that I was going to bury my son without any knowledge of who murdered him. That is always a mother's fear—to not have a clue on who murdered their child. Thank you so much, Sinclair."

Mrs. Kathryn goes on to tell Sinclair that she has been to the hospital to see Kenneth's body and that they are taking the body to the mortuary on Monday, so they can make preparations for the funeral on Saturday. "He looked as if he was at peace," she says. "All I could do was smile and think about all the times Kenneth used to tell me how he was going to buy me this big house once he made it to the NBA. And now my baby is gone for the price of a lousy thousand dollars. I hope that they find those boys, and when they do, I want to ask them why they killed my son." Sinclair hears the hurt in Mrs. Kathryn's voice and tires to reassure her, "It's going to be ok."

"I just don't understand how people can be so hateful," says Mrs. Kathryn. After she calms down a bit, she begins to tell Sinclair about going to the mortuary to see her son and choose the casket for him. Eager to see Kenneth again, Sinclair asks Mrs. Kathryn if it would be alright for her to come along with her. Mrs. Kathryn happily agrees and gives her the time to meet her there. After making the arrangements, they end the conversation and hang up the phone.

After about thirty minutes on the phone with Mrs. Kathryn, Sinclair's body suddenly shuts down on her, as she is very tired from the events that took place since last night. She lays quietly on her bed and falls asleep. While she is sleeping, Grandma and Tiffany are downstairs preparing dinner. Uncle Pete is still on the porch, now drinking a beer. Grandma is making her special macaroni and cheese recipe.

She asks Tiffany to get her two eggs from the refrigerator and some milk. Along with the three cheeses she uses, she mixes all the ingredients together. She then prepares her collard greens, potato salad, homemade apple pie, deep fried chicken, and her specialty signature drink—sweet tea.

As the food is cooking, Grandma and Tiffany go to the front porch to join Uncle Pete. Tiffany runs to the front yard and grabs her jump rope. "Is the food ready?" asks Uncle Pete. "No," says Grandma. "It will be in about an hour from now. I can't wait until all this is over," she says as they watch Tiffany jumping rope happily.

An hour and a half goes by and Grandma, Uncle Pete and Tiffany are preparing the dinner table. Christy and Jana have arrived. "Tiffany, go upstairs and get Sinclair please," says Grandma. "Yes ma'm." Uncle Pete invites Christy and Jana to come inside. "How are you feeling?" asks Uncle Pete. "I'm doing fine," Christy replies. "What about you Jana?" Jana pauses with a frustrated look on her face.

"We know what happened to you last night. That bastard is going to get what he deserves," says Uncle Pete. Jana tells him that she is feeling better but regrets putting herself in that situation. "I should have known better and not gotten to the point I was in." "It was a mistake for you to be drinking as much as you you did, but there is no excuse for him raping you," says Grandma.

"Did you go to the hospital to get checked out?" "No ma'm." "You need to do that as soon as possible, so that you can know if there's anything wrong with you. There is no wondering what that man has." They all nod in agreement with Grandma. Sinclair is awakened by Tiffany to come downstairs to join everybody else for dinner.

As they are coming downstairs, Sinclair is alerted by her favorite food scents in the air. "Smells like mac and cheese, greens, chicken, and homemade apple pie," she says. Sinclair sits down at the table, feeling fully revived and relaxed. "You look great," says Grandma. "That nap did you some good." "I really needed that," Sinclair agrees. "Well, hello ladies," she says, turning to Christy and Jana. "How long have y'all been here?"

"We arrived about ten minutes ago," Jana replies. "We were not going to miss your Grandma's coking for anything in the world," adds Christy. Before they begin to eat, Grandma asks Uncle Pete to say the grace. "Bless the food," she says to him. Because of the circumstances and the grief the events that took place last night brought upon them, Uncle Pete tells them that he would like to do something a little different.

Instead of sitting down and saying grace, he tells everyone to stand up and holds hands. "Bow your heads," he instructs and, when they do, he begins to say a prayer.

"Dear Lord, we thank you for this food we are about to receive. We thank you for all the blessing that you have bestowed upon us. We ask you to forgive our sins as we repent them to you. We fear you, Lord, so we ask that you have mercy on our souls. We have lost a dear friend of the family, Kenneth, and we ask you to bless his soul, and forgive his sins. We also ask of you to forgive the men that have committed this sin to him. Bless his mother and bring strength to her heart. We thank you again; in Jesus' name, Amen."

After that, everybody sits down and starts to have dinner. "This looks and smells good," says Jana. "I am so hungry," says Christy. "Eat as much as your stomach can hold. There's plenty of food here for everybody," says Grandma. "Tiffany, for desert, I am going to add your favorite ice cream to go along with that homemade apple pie I made." As food is passed around, all that can be heard is the sound of silverware and plates.

It's an hour later and conversation starts to pick back up. "I am so stuffed," says Jana. "Me too," adds Christy. "That was the best macaroni and cheese I've ever had," Christy compliments Grandma. "Thanks, Mrs. Hart, for a great dinner," Christy and Jana say in unison. "You girls are welcome to join our family for dinner anytime," says Grandma. "Even when Sinclair moves to Atlanta, you girls are still welcome," she adds.

"Oh, about Atlanta, we have decided that we are going to join you in the journey," says Christy. Sinclair stares at Christy with a stunned and surprised look on her face. "Stop playing," she says. "We are so serious," says Jana. "With all this stuff taking place, we just need to pack up and leave with you," adds Christy. "There's nothing here for us and going to Atlanta sounds like the perfect plan," says Jana.

"I agree with you girls," says Grandma. "By the way, you don't need to go to that big city by yourself. At least you will have two of your best friends there to navigate with you there," she adds.

Jana and Christy are due to graduate this summer from Howard University as well. So, after the graduation ceremony takes place in August, they would be ready to join Sinclair in her move to Atlanta. Sinclair agrees and the girls are filled with joy.

"Grandma, since you have cooked this amazing meal today, we will do the dishes and put everything away," says Sinclair. "Yes momma, the girls will do the cleaning," agrees Uncle Pete, laughing as he is heading out the door. "Where are you going?" asks Sinclair. "I have some errands to run before I go to work tomorrow." "Are you not going to help us clean up?" "I could, but three is already a crowd. You ladies have a goodnight and thanks momma for a great meal."

He gives his mother a kiss and leaves the house. Grandma heads upstairs telling the girls goodnight, as she thanks them for being so kind to clean the kitchen. The girls wish her goodnight and start cleaning the kitchen. "Your grandmother is so sweet," says Jana. "I am going to miss both of them; well, actually, all three of them when I am gone," says Sinclair, referring to Grandma, Uncle Pete, and Tiffany.

"By the way, did you tell your mother what happened to you Jana?" asks Sinclair. "No I didn't. I know how she gets when something bad happens to me and I just didn't want to hear all of that stuff right now." "But that's your mom," says Christy. "Look I'm just going to hope for the best and hope that the cops find Chris." Jana goes on to recap what happened that night and said to Sinclair and Christy, "He didn't even have the courtesy to wear a condom." "Oh my God!" shouts Sinclair.

"He didn't wear a condom?" "No," says Jana. "There's no telling how many girls he has done this to," says Sinclair. "I know that this sounds bad and stuff, but do you know if he pulled out?" asks Christy. "I don't think that he did," she responds in a daze, trying to remember what happened. "All I remember is him getting up and going to the bathroom once he was finished." "Let's hope that you don't get pregnant by that fool," says Sinclair.

"Don't speak that on me. That would be a terrible thing for me to go through," says Jana. "I will pray that you are not pregnant from this incident." After the girls finish cleaning up Grandma's kitchen, they go into the living room to watch some television. As they are flipping through the channels, they come across the local news station. "Wait, they are talking about the last night's shooting," shouts Christy. "Turn it up!" urges Jana.

The girls sit back to watch and hear what the news reporter has to say about the case.

"There has been a murder homicide at the Waffle House here, late last night, around 2 am. The victim was the All American guard Kenneth Daniels from the University of Maryland. The police is said to have Derrick Spaulding as a possible suspect in the murder. They also have an arrest warrant for Chris

Spaulding and James Dunn as two other suspects. Derrick is being released on $500,000 bond."

The girls listen to the reporter in more detail as she continues to comment on the homicide that took place last night. The news station flashes photos of Kenneth, Derrick, and James on the television screen. "I Derrick must be upset with me for getting him into this mess," says Sinclair. "Look, you were just looking out for the best interest of Kenneth," says Christy. "Still, you had no idea that Derrick had anything to do with his murder," Jana disagrees.

"He said that he would call you when he is released, so just wait until then to talk to him. And, as I said, Mike told me that he was getting out today," Christy suggests. "I guess, I will wait until he calls me." "Look, they are talking to Kenneth's mother on the news," shouts Christy. "When I talked to her earlier, she didn't mention to me that she was going to be on the news," says Sinclair.

The girls quit down, so they can hear Mrs. Kathryn, as she begins to tell the news reporter that whoever is responsible for her son's death needs to turn their selves in. She goes on to say that if they have any remorse regarding their part in the death of her child, that they need to come forth. "It's hard for me and my family to rest until we know who is responsible for his death," she says to the reporter.

You can feel the tension in her voice, as Mrs. Kathryn, starts to tear up during her statement. "I really hope they catch those guys so that Mrs. Kathryn can be at peace," says Sinclair. The news reporter concludes the report by saying that, if the viewers have any knowledge of where the two suspects Chris and James are, they should contact the police immediately, adding that Chris Spaulding is armed and dangerous.

Sinclair and Christy get a call from Derrick and Mike five minutes after the news programme finishes. "This is Derrick," she says after looking at her phone. "Mike is calling me too," notes Christy. As they answer their phones, Christy takes her call in the kitchen, so that she can talk to Mike in private. "Hey Sinclair," says Derrick. "Hey," she responds. "Where are you?" "I'm at the hotel." "Look, I just want to apologize to you for the mix up. I didn't have time to think and didn't find out what really happened until we met up with Jana," she says. "Look, I understand. It's just now I got to deal with all this media attention and the NFL Commissioner getting into my business. And to make matters worse, I have a sore knee. I've just been traded, and I haven't signed my contract yet. Damn, what am I going to do?"

"All of this is going to pass eventually, and you will be in the clear shortly." "Let's hope so." Derrick apologizes to Sinclair about what happened between him and Kenneth and says that he didn't mean that he would kill Kenneth for real. "I was just upset at the fact that my football career was over. I would never do anything to hurt anybody unless it's on the football field." "I know," she reassures him.

He goes on to explain how he knows that she had been through a lot and that losing her boyfriend was bad enough, but insists that he wanted to get to know her. "I've liked you the very first time I saw you that night at the Pool Hall. I want us to get to know each other." "Derrick, I know that you have good intentions, but right now is not the time to talk about us getting to know each other. I just lost my boyfriend and I'm in no rush at all to get involved with anybody else. If the circumstances were different, then maybe. But right now is not the time.

Derrick agrees and apologizes for pressuring her. "Well, I have to call my agent. I guess, when you are feeling better, give me a call. I have to be in Atlanta for minicamp in a week, so you can reach me after that." Sinclair agrees and they end the call. She goes back into the living room where Jana and Christy are waiting to hear about her conversation. "So what did he say to you?" asks Jana. "We both apologized and I told him that, at this time, I wasn't looking to date anybody," says Sinclair.

"It's seems as if he doesn't understand what is going on and that all he can think about is his career and us getting to know each other. Now that Kenneth is dead, I am going to take a much needed break away from any relationship." "Same for me! I'm not going to trust anybody for a long time after what I have been through," Jana agrees.

It's Monday and Sinclair is due to meet Mrs. Kathryn at the mortuary. She arrives at 2:05 pm to see Mrs. Kathryn's car already parked outside. She gets out of her car and runs inside. "Hello Mrs. Kathryn, sorry for being late." "It's not a problem," she replies. The two women are waiting for the funeral director to appear. "It's so scary being around all these coffins," says Sinclair. "Don't be afraid, baby. We all have to die someday."

The funeral director approaches them. "Hello Mrs. Kathryn. I want to send my deepest prayers out to your family." "Thank you," she responds. "We are having too many black on black crimes mostly involving our young adults. They are coming to us by the dozen. I wouldn't be surprised if I get two more today," he says jokingly.

Mrs. Kathryn and Sinclair look at the funeral director, clearly not amused by his joke. "Ok, we are here to talk business, so let's get down to it," Mrs. Kathryn suggests, interrupting his inappropriate joking. She gives the funeral director all the details on how she wants Kenneth's funeral arrangements to proceed. She explains to him that she wants him to be buried in a cherry wood coffin with a white bedded interior. She tells him that he should be wearing a black suite, black shoes, a white button down collar shirt, and a black tie. With everything in order, they leave the funeral home.

It's Saturday, the day of Kenneth's funeral. "Well, the day has finally come to bury him," says Sinclair. Grandma looks at Sinclair and reminds her to try to be strong, telling her that Kenneth is in a better place and that he shall be a piece. After the arrival of Christy, Jana, and Uncle Pete, they leave Grandma's house and gets into Sinclair and Christy car.

Ten minutes later, they arrive to the church, at the other side of town, noticing hundreds of people in attendance for the funeral. Even some of Kenneth's high school and college basketball teammates came to attend his funeral. They pile up into the church. The choir is singing and you can hear the sounds of Amen throughout the audience. The pastor speaks on behalf of Kenneth to tell what he knows of him. He says;

> *"And now, dear children, remain in fellowship with Christ, so that when he returns, you will be full of courage and not shrink back from his shame. Since we know that Christ is righteous, we also know that all who do what is right are God's children!" John 1 2: 28-29*

After many in attendance spoke of Kenneth, it was time to move to the burial grounds, where he was to be laid to rest. "I want to thank each and every one of you for attending today's ceremony," says Mrs. Kathryn. "I'm sure Kenneth is looking down and smiling to see all of you here today." After Mrs. Kathryn gives her last speech, the pastor tells everyone to bow their heads, as he prays. He ends the prayer by saying, "May this young man rest in peace." Down goes the coffin.

CHAPTER 5

It has been a couple of weeks since Kenneth's funeral and everybody is trying to get on with their lives. Christy and Jana are back at Summer School at Howard University to graduate in August and Sinclair is about a month away from leaving to go to Atlanta. In the meantime, she begins to volunteer at a nearby homeless shelter to take her mind off everything that has taken place within the last few weeks. While at the shelter, she meets Mrs. Taylor, the director of the shelter, as well as a therapist.

"Hello, my name is Mrs. Taylor." "My name is Sinclair and I am here to volunteer at the shelter." "Welcome aboard. Are you ready to make a huge difference in someone's life?" "Yes, but I think someone needs to make a big difference in my life too." "What's that supposed to mean?" "I don't know if I should bring my personal business into your place of business" "This may be a homeless shelter, but this shelter is also a place where people can bring their frustrations in and get them off their chest."

Sinclair stares at Mrs. Taylor, wondering if she should share her recent experiences with a woman she just met. "Let me formally introduce myself and tell you a little about me," offers Mrs. Taylor, sensing Sinclair's indecision. "I want you to feel as comfortable possible. My name is Angela Taylor and I am thirty two years old, and a mother of two beautiful kids. I attended the University of Virginia and graduated with an MBA in Psychology."

She continues to tell Sinclair as much as she needed too so that she could feel a little more comfortable with her. "I could tell the first time I saw you that you were a woman that had a lot on her mind. I have been around many young women, and I know when they have something on their minds. So, whenever you are ready to talk, feel free to come to me," Mrs. Taylor concludes, smiling at Sinclair warmly.

Sinclair is pleased to hear that Mrs. Taylor is there if she needs to vent. "Well, until then, I have a few people to go and check on." She then tells Sinclair that they will have lunch together and if she wants to take the opportunity to talk, that she would be open to hear anything she needs to get off her chest. In the meantime, Sinclair is asked to get familiar with the shelter and meet some of the homeless people.

"I have never seen so many people in need," Sinclair notes to herself. She begins to feel very sorry for those that are so unfortunate that tears start welling up in her eyes. "Look at the mothers with their little children!" she says. "Here I am worried about my situation, and these are people that need the most help."

Sinclair goes through every room that the shelter has, meeting and greeting all the occupants. "This is my calling. How could so many people on our streets be overlooked and not get the help that they deserve? I am going to do my best to make a difference in someone's life," she says, her voice full of newfound resolve.

Sinclair sees a woman with her young infant. "Hello," she greets her. The lady stares at Sinclair looking very emotional. "God did this to me," the lady says. "He punished me for all the wrong I've done." "No, no; God will never do this. May I sit down and talk with you?" she asks the lady. With no response from the lady, Sinclair sits down next to her.

"How did this happen to you?" "Do you really want to know, or you are just trying to be nice?" "I would really love to know your story, if you are willing to share it with me." The lady lays her baby down on the bed and looks at Sinclair. She grabs her hands. "Look at me; I never thought in my life that I would be in this situation. I am thirty years old and drugs have taken over my life. Let me tell you my story," she says to Sinclair.

She stares at the lady, sincerely interested in her life story. "When I was in high school, I was the most popular girl there. I had all the boys wanting me and all the girls hating me. I was a cheerleader and I was homecoming queen. I remember the one mistake I made." "What mistake was that?" "The most popular guy in school was this big drug dealer and I was so attracted to him."

She goes on to tell Sinclair about the nice car he drove and the nice clothes he would wear and how all the girls wanted him. "I remember stepping out of mu comfort zone to talk to this guy, who was surprisingly quite a gentleman." She pauses briefly to introduce herself to Sinclair. "By the way, my name is Karen." She then continues to tell her about the ride she took with the guy.

"One day, after school, he asks me to come and ride with him. At first, I was a little nervous, but as I said, he had a way with words. I get into the car with him and we leave the school grounds." Karen goes on to say how the guy seemed so interested and how he had been paying attention to her for such a long time. "I feel for all his game. Anyway, one day I was with him and we were at his place and he offered me a drink. I never had a drink in my life, so I refused at first, but he soon made me feel as if everything was going to be ok," she says.

"I took the drink and started feeling lightheaded. Because the feeling was so unusual to me, I wanted more and more. As I requested it, he gladly gave me more. After the drink, he rolled up some weed and we started smoking it. I got so high that I passed out. The next morning, I woke up naked in his bed. I realized at that moment that I had done something really stupid. To make matters worse, it was a school day and I didn't attend," she says.

"I asked him why was I naked in his bed and he told me that we had sex. That was the very first time I had sex. I was shocked that the guy I barely knew was my first and I could not even remember it. I got out of bed and saw the blood all over his sheets. Although I did feel badly, he reassured me that everything was still ok. I got dressed and he drove me home. Whatever he gave me must have started to take control of my mind."

"I started wanting more and more of what he gave me that day. As weeks pass by, I could see the change in my behavior. I was cutting classes, my grades were deteriorating, and I didn't have the energy to cheer anymore. After a while, my addiction got so bad that he started forcing me have sex with his friends in exchange for drugs. I still graduated from high school that year, but because of my bad grades, I lost my scholarship."

"My parents didn't have much money to give me to go to school, so I had to hustle my way to pay for further education. To make matters worse, I got pregnant. Because of the many different guys I've slept with, I didn't really know who the baby's father was. I ended up getting an abortion. I had to come up with quick way to get some money, so I started stripping in clubs. The stripping turned to prostitution."

"After doing that for many years, my body was out of shape. The looks I did have in high school were long gone. Nobody wanted to mess with me. I got so depressed that I wanted to kill myself. I started taking and using many different drugs. At that time in my life, I was a junkie. I lost both of my parents at the age of twenty five and had no one to turn to."

"Because of my reputation, I could no longer stay in my hometown. So I moved to D.C. and then here to Baltimore. So this shelter is all that I have." Karen looks at her baby. "This is my baby, she is six months old." "Where is the father?" asks Sinclair. "I was raped and wanted to keep the baby because I didn't want to be alone." After Sinclair hears Karen's story, she bursts into tears. "Everything is going to be ok. You may think that God has done this to you, but he didn't. God has a plan for you."

Sinclair and Karen give each other a hug and Sinclair promises Karen that she would see her again. Karen smiles and tells her goodbye. Sinclair leaves the room and continues acknowledging and speaking to many other homeless people. The story that Karen just told her seems to outweigh every other story she hears in a shelter. She now feels very open minded to discuss her problem with Mrs. Taylor.

It's now 12 o'clock and Sinclair is on her way to lunch with Mrs. Taylor. She meets up with Mrs. Taylor at Red Lobster. "So how is everything going?" she asks Sinclair. "Fine." "Did you talk to any of the shelter occupants?" "Yes, to many. However, one in particular stood out for me." "And who was that?" "I met a young lady named Karen and she talked to me about how she ended up in the shelter. I was so touched by her story that it made me cry. I thought that I was going through so much, but I now realize that my problems are nothing compared to theirs."

"Why do you say that?" "I mean, look at me. I just graduated from college and am about to move to Atlanta, I have great health and am surrounded by people that love me, and I'm complaining about small things. How selfish can a person be?" "Just because your problems are small, doesn't mean that you can't talk about them and try to address them. It's true that everybody goes through problems in life, but the strong survive. Karen's situation is no different from anybody else's, including yours."

"I just want to help people like her." "You can't help any-body until you help yourself." When Mrs. Taylor says that, Sinclair looks at her, realizing that she needed to hear someone tell her that. "Now since we got that all out the way, what is your situation?" asks Mrs. Taylor. Sinclair proceeds to tell Mrs. Taylor about the shooting that took place a few weeks ago and about her family situation, including the death of her mother.

"So how does losing your mother at such young age make you feel?" asks Mrs. Taylor. "My mother died when I was fifteen years old. I knew that she had problems, but she always made time for me and my little sister," says Sinclair. "So you have a younger sister?" "Yes, but we have different fathers." "What problems did your mother have?" "My mother was a heavy drug user and had a real hard time trying to stay clean."

"She was never really high around us, but I knew from her body language that she was an addict. My grandmother took me in at a very young age because of my mother's addiction. I don't know what I would do if I didn't have my grandmother," says Sinclair. "And your mother, did someone kill her?" "No, she died from a drug overdose."

As Sinclair continues to answer questions that Mrs. Taylor is asking, she starts to get really emotional. "I am so sorry that you are feeling this way. If you don't want to talk about this anymore, we can stop," says Mrs. Taylor. "No, it's not a problem. I need to vent and get this off my chest.

After eating and discussing the challenges Sinclair has been through, Mrs. Taylor notices the time and advises that they need to get back to the shelter. "When we get back to my office, if nothing needs our urgent attention, we could finish our conversation." The two of them get into their cars and head back to the shelter. On the way back, Sinclair is listening to the radio, as they are talking about the upcoming NBA Draft, Kenneth's absence and the impact it will have on the draft class that's coming out.

After hearing a few more minutes of the conversation, overwhelmed, she turns the radio off and starts crying. Back at the shelter, Mrs. Taylor and Sinclair make some more rounds to check on the staff and the inhabitants. "Everything seems to be in order," Mrs. Taylor says. Sinclair, eager to know how the shelter functions, asks Mrs. Taylor some questions. "What are the procedures here?" "First, you have to be either homeless or battered women to be taken into the shelter," she responds.

"We try not to turn away anybody with the right attitude. Still, because of the limited space, most homeless come in for meals, showers, haircuts, and maybe a bed, if some are available. Everybody checks out the next morning and if they need to come back, they are welcomed." "That's great," says Sinclair. "When I make it big, I promise myself that I am going to make a difference in someone's life," she adds.

"You don't have to wait until you make it, you can start now with what you are doing." "You are right." "Ok, is there anything else that you would like to tell me?" asks Mrs. Taylor. "I would like to tell you about my friend Jana." "What about her?" "Jana was raped by this guy and because of it, she seems to be a little antisocial, and I know that she acts that way because she is really hurt by her experience." "You know, many people hide their hurt by denying the fact that it happened so they don't have to deal with the pain."

"We tried to get her to go to the hospital, better yet, tell her parents, but she refuses to do either," Sinclair explains. Mrs. Taylor goes on to tell Sinclair the reason that Jana is afraid to be open about her rape. "Firstly, she has to be comfortable doing those things. You can't make a person do something that they don't want to do. That only pushes them farther away from doing it. Does she know the person that raped her?" "Yes, some guy name Chris Spaulding."

"Are you sure the name is Chris Spaulding?" "Yes, I am sure." "That name sounds familiar." "The police have a warrant for his arrest." "Good! So she did press charges?" "Yes," says Sinclair. "What about you?" asks Mrs. Taylor. "You are telling me about your friend, but what do you want to tell me about you?"

Sinclair goes on to tell her about her boyfriend Kenneth and the situation that took place a few weeks ago. "My boyfriend was shot and killed by this guy Chris that raped Jana. That night, he committed both crimes." "Oh my God, this guy Chris is terrible and I hope that they catch him really soon." Mrs. Taylor goes on to tell Sinclair that she heard about the shooting and the murder but wouldn't have thought that she was a part of that.

"I feel so badly for your loss," she says. "I'm learning to get over it, but it's going to take me some time. What makes it so difficult for me is that we had this huge argument earlier on the day of his murder. He got into this fight with Derrick, a guy I met that night, and got very angry at me for that. The last words that he said to me were to meet him at the Waffle House, so that we could talk.

But as soon as we pulled up, five minutes later we heard gun shots and Kenneth was dead. I just feel so responsible for his death." "It's not your fault. Things happen for a reason." After talking with Mrs. Taylor, Sinclair leaves her office, finishes her work at the shelter and heads home.

As Sinclair gets inside the house, she is greeted by her grandma. "How was your first day at the shelter?" "It was fine; I met some really interesting people today." Sinclair tells Grandma about the day at the shelter and Karen. "How did that make you feel?" "I was very saddened by her story, but it made me feel a little better about the experience that I just went through."

Sinclair goes on to say how she met the shelter's director and how she was able to open up about her life to her. "You're talking about Mrs. Taylor," say Grandma. "Yes, how did you know her name?" "Years ago, before your mother passed away, I knew her mother. Mrs. Taylor's mother was the one that took your mother Cynthia into the shelter. Your mother was there many days, trying to get help, but whenever she left, she would have a relapse."

"Wow, I didn't know that. Why didn't you tell me this earlier Grandma?" "You had such a tough time already that I didn't want to add to your frustrations." "I guess that's another topic Mrs. Taylor and I will have when I go back there tomorrow." After a few minutes talking to Grandma, she goes upstairs to change her clothes and Grandma tells her that dinner will be ready in thirty minutes.

After she gets dressed, she gets a call from Jana. "Hey girl," Jana greets her. "Just getting back in from the shelter; How's is the campus life?" "I am so ready to graduate so that we can leave for Atlanta. The waiting is killing me," Jana replies. "You only have a few weeks, so hang in there, girl!" "If only I didn't take that stupid semester off, I would have graduated with you." "See what that playing will do for you. If you play now, you're going to suffer later," says Sinclair.

After a few minutes on the phone, Jana remembers the real reason for calling Sinclair. "I got a call from Chris the other day." "Are you serious?" "Yes, but I didn't answer the phone and he kept ringing. What should I do if he calls again?" "You need to report it to the police in D.C. so they can catch up with him." "Girl, I am so scared to leave my apartment," says Jana.

"Well, you have to do something before it drives you crazy." "I have an idea; I will just change my number so I want receive any calls from here anymore." "You do that, but in the meantime, don't answer his calls," says Sinclair. Jana agrees to do just that and almost forgets to tell Sinclair one more important detail. "I have something else to tell you." "Please can it be less dramatic than what you just told me?" "I don't think so, but here it goes," responds Jana. "I think that I'm pregnant."

Sinclair is shocked and remains quiet for a few minutes after she hears the news. "How do you know?" "I haven't had my period yet and it's been three weeks." You need to find out if you are really pregnant," says Sinclair. "If you are, what are you going to do?" she asks. "There's no way that I am having this baby," Jana says.

"I will burn in hell before I have a murderer's baby. What would you do?" she asks Sinclair. "No matter what the circumstances are, I just don't believe in abortions." "Even if you have been raped?" Jana asks, somewhat shocked by her friend's view. "I've been raped, and I cannot bring myself raise murderer's child." says Jana.

Jana gets a little frustrated at how Sinclair is taking this and at the moment refuses to hear her out. "All I am saying, Jana, is that no matter what the situation is, a child is a blessing from God," Sinclair says. "And if God didn't want you to have this baby, you wouldn't be pregnant," she adds. "I understand where you are coming from with all that religion, but I want to have a relationship with my child's father, and I want be having one with no damn Chris," she retorts angrily.

"I am not telling you that you have to keep the baby, I'm just telling you what I would do if it was me." "Yeah right, and I would love to see that, if this happens to you, you would be a woman of your word," adds Jana.

After a few more minutes on the phone with Jana, Sinclair hears a call from Grandma telling her to get Tiffany and come downstairs to have dinner. She tells Jana that they will discuss her situation later. On the way downstairs, Sinclair can smell the food. "This is another favorite of mine!" she notes, looking forward to the dinner that Grandma is prepared—the meatloaf, mashed potatoes, mixed vegetables, and homemade cornbread.

"Where is Uncle Pete?" asks Sinclair. "Pete had to work late tonight, so he want be joining us for dinner," says Grandma. Sinclair, Grandma, and Tiffany sit down to enjoy their dinner and, afterwards, Sinclair helps Grandma put away the dishes. She can't help but tell her the news she got from Jana earlier. "Jana thinks that she is pregnant," she says.

Grandma is the type of person that has a vibe about any and everything around her. She is truly blessed. "I dreamed of fish," she said. "That is how I knew that someone was pregnant but, I didn't know who. So if the young lady is expecting, what is she going to do about it?" "She is so convinced that she is going to get rid of the baby by having an abortion," says Sinclair.

"Well everybody is entitled to their own decisions, and if she feels having an abortion is the best for her, then that's her decision." "How do you feel about abortions?" Sinclair asks. "If it was up to me, then I would be against it, but it's not, and in her situation and considering how it happened, I can understand why she wants to have the abortion," says Grandma. After a few minutes of discussion, Sinclair and Grandma finish the dishes and head upstairs for the rest of the night.

The next day comes and Sinclair decides to go back to the shelter and volunteer again. "Welcome back," Mrs. Taylor greets her. Sinclair follows Mrs. Taylor into her office to see if she could speak with her. "May I have a word with you?"

"Why, of course," Mrs. Taylor reassures her. "I was speaking to my Grandmother yesterday and she told me that your mother knew mine." "What was your mother's name?" asks Mrs. Taylor. "Cynthia, Cynthia Hart."

Mrs. Taylor pulls the files to locate Sinclair's mother's name. "Oh yes, here it is," she says. "I see that your mother had been here quite a few times." "Yes, apparently she visited the shelter often. My grandma said that she was under the care of your mother."

For a few more minutes, they continue to talk about the connection between Sinclair's grandma and Mrs. Taylor's mother. Mrs. Taylor feels that she need to share with Sinclair some important information regarding the conversation they had yesterday. "I have something to tell you about what we talked about yesterday." With a puzzled look on her face, Sinclair sits to the edge of her seat, curious to know what Mrs. Taylor has to tell her.

"You were telling me about this guy named Chris Spaulding, who killed your boyfriend and raped your friend," she says. "Yes, what about him?" she says. "Well, that guy Chris is my cousin and he is responsible for the rape of the young lady Karen you were talking to yesterday." Sinclair was in shock after she heard the news. "When she came to the shelter, she was just as open as you to get everything off her chest, so she told me everything that happened to her," says Mrs. Taylor. "Why didn't you say anything?" "I needed to get more information first and then I was going to find the time to tell you, and this is the time."

"I stopped associated myself with him once he started taking and dealing drugs. Chris has been in and out of jail since a very young age. His own family members have distanced themselves from him." Sinclair and Mrs. Taylor talk a few more minutes about Chris and decide to come up with a plan to get him to the police.

"I have an idea," says Sinclair. "Since he is on the run from the police, he is not going to trust many people," says Mrs. Taylor. "Give me a few minutes to put everything together." Sinclair gets her cell phone and calls Jana. She informs Jana of the things that Mrs. Taylor had mentioned to her and that she has a plan to connect the police with Chris.

Before she gives her the plan, Jana tells Sinclair that, indeed, she is pregnant, as she had just taken a home pregnancy test. "That's even better," says Sinclair. "Here is what we are going to do. I need you to call Chris and tell him that you are pregnant and ask him to meet you at your place so y'all can maybe talk about being together," she suggests.

"After he gives you the time, we notify the police where y'all are at." "What if he thinks that I'm trying to set him up?" "He will at first, but you have to make it convincing that you want to be with him, and tell him that you will tell the police that you were with him the night of the shooting if he does not agree to meet you," Sinclair explains. "Just make it seem real as possible, so that he doesn't suspect anything," she says.

"We will alert the police of the things that you are going to tell them when you are around Chris," says Sinclair. After she gets Jana to agree to go through with the plan, Sinclair calls Detective Williams and Detective Smith to tell them of the latest developments. She picks up her cell phone and makes the call. "Hello," says Detective Williams. "This is Sinclair and we have a plan to catch Chris for you." "How do you plan on doing that?"

After she explains the plan in detail, the detective calmly accepts the idea. After she gets off the phone with the detective, she calls Jana back and tells her to go ahead and set up a time for Chris to meet her at her place. Jana calls Chris. "Hey how are you?" she asks. "You know, the police are looking for me," he says. "All because you told them that I shot your friend's boyfriend that night."

"First of all, I didn't tell them that you had shot him. My friends must have told them. I didn't tell them anything. I didn't want them to know about what happened with me. If they do come after you, I will gladly tell them that I was with you all night." "Why would you do that for me?" he asks. "Because I am pregnant and you are the father," she replies.

Not stunned at all, Chris responds to Jana, "What does that have to do with me? That doesn't mean anything to me." Barely keeping her composure, Jana tells Chris that she would want them to be together and raise the baby as a family despite what he just said. After some persuasion, Chris is beginning to believe what Jana is saying.

"So, can we meet at my place to talk about this in person?" asks Jana. "How do I know that you are going to be alone?" "If you don't trust me, you can pick me up." Chris agrees to pick her up in about an hour. Jana quickly calls Sinclair back to give her all the details of the arrangements that they have made.

"Chris is coming to pick me up in an hour. He also told me that he would be driving a black Ford Explorer," she says. Sinclair takes the information down and calls the detective. After getting the information, Detective Williams and Detective Smith get into their car and drive to Jana's place. When they arrive, they stake out in the parking lot are to wait on Chris arrival.

After about forty-five minutes, they spot a black Ford Explorer pulling up to the apartment complex parking lot. Chris calls Jana from his cell phone to let her know that he is outside. Not knowing if that's Chris or not, the detectives wait until they see Jana approach the SUV. Five minutes later, Jana comes walking outside. Chris is still sitting in his car waiting for Jana to get in.

As Jana approaches the SUV, the detectives jump out on Chris. "Get out of the car, get out of the car!" they yell with guns pointed at Chris. Chris laughs, surprised that he was caught so easily. The detectives pull him out of the car, handcuff him and put him in the back of the squad car. "You did it!" Detective Williams congratulates Jana.

Jana calls Sinclair to inform them that Chris has been arrested. Sinclair and Mrs. Taylor are overwhelmed that Kenneth's killer has been caught. Sinclair quickly calls Kenneth's mom, Mrs. Kathryn, to tell her the news. Mrs.

Kathryn begins to cry. "That's the best news I've heard since they buried my baby."

"Thank you Mrs. Taylor," says Sinclair. "No, thank you," she replies. "If it weren't for you telling me your situation, I would have never known that the guy was my cousin Chris." "I will never forget you when I'm in Atlanta," says Sinclair. They give each other a hug and Sinclair heads back to her grandmother's house to deliver the good news.

On her way home, she gets a call from Derrick. Sinclair tells him what just happened. "I know," says Derrick. "I just got a call from my attorney, saying that the charges had been dropped." "That's awesome!" she replies. "Is that the only reason you called me?" "I also want to tell you that I miss talking to you and that I can't wait to see you in Atlanta soon," he says. With a smile from cheek to cheek, Sinclair tells him that she can't wait to see him either.

On her way home, Sinclair remembers a scripture her grandmother used to recite and she begins to say it out loud to herself.

> "The Lord is my rock, my fortress, and my savior; my God is my rock, in who I find protection. He is my shield, the power that saves me, and my place of safety. He is my refuge, my savior, the one who saves me from violence. I called on the Lord, who is worthy of praise, and he saved me from my enemies." Samuel 2, 22:3-4

The end of the summer is approaching and it's time for the girls to move to Atlanta. Grandma has organized a big cookout for the girls going away party. Uncle Pete is on the grill, in charge of cooking the meat. Christy and Jana had completed their studies at Howard University. Everybody had stopped by to see the girls off.

Mrs. Kathryn, Mrs. Taylor, and even Detective Williams and Detective Smith, all stop by their cookout. "Are you ready?" Sinclair asks Christy. "You know that I'm," Christy responds. "What about you Jana?" "I am one hundred percent ready." "Are you ready Sinclair?" they both asks her. "With everything that has taken place over the summer, I am more than ready to go make new positive memories," she says.

"I hate to see my girls go, but they are young women now and they have to make a living of their own," says Grandma. As the cookout continues, Mrs. Kathryn pulls Sinclair aside. "I know losing Kenneth was a huge loss in your life, but promise me, baby, that you are going to move on with your life and not let his death hold you back. Understand that my son is gone and you have to live your life."

Sinclair looks into Mrs. Kathryn's eyes almost tearing up. "I will always miss him, but I know that he would want me to be happy." They give each other a hug and join the crowd as Sinclair, Christy, and Jana start chanting, "ATL, ATL, ATL!"

CHAPTER 6

ATLANTA, GEORGIA

After many hours of driving, the girls finally arrive in Atlanta—the city they now call home. With their cars loaded with many items and a large U-Haul truck trailing behind, the girls make their way to their apartments. "I am so glad we got that part out of the way," says Sinclair." "We brought everything except the kitchen sink," says Jana. "After ten hours on the road, I need to take a well deserved nap," says Christy.

"I am so glad we hired some movers to help us unload this stuff because, if I had to do it, it wouldn't get done," says Sinclair. The girls, looking really exhausted, goes to the leasing office to meet with the property manager. After about an hour of looking at their apartments and signing the lease agreements, the girls are given their keys to their respective new homes. Sinclair's apartment is located near the front of the apartment community, and Jana's is in the back, with Christy's apartment in the middle.

"Damn girl, I am going to have to have to take a bus just to come and see your ass way in the back," Sinclair jokes. "That's fine, it will just limit y'all bitches from wearing out you're welcome," Jana retorts. "At least, y'all are on the second floor; my apartment is located on the first," she adds. "I am going to be getting my exercise every time I leave to go somewhere," says Jana.

After several minutes of humorous complaining, the girls get serious and begin the next step in officially becoming residents of Atlanta. They begin to unpack and get situated. Five hours later, it is Saturday evening, and the girls have managed to get their belongings into some order. With majority of the furniture belonging to Sinclair, Christy and Jana really didn't have much to unload, which allowed them to help Sinclair move.

"I am starving," Christy starts to complain, now truly exhausted. "Now that we got this out the way, I think it's time to go out and get familiar with the city," says Jana. "First we need to take a shower and then we can worry about finding something to eat," says Sinclair. The girls take about an hour to shower and change clothes. They all meet back up at Sinclair's place to decide what to do next.

"Hey, since we really don't know where we are going, let's go ask one of the ladies in the leasing office if they have some helpful suggestions for us," Sinclair suggests. They leave the apartment and go back to the leasing office for some help in planning their first outing in Atlanta. "Hello ladies. Did y'all get everything settled in?" asks the Property Manager. "So far so good," Sinclair responds. "How can I help y'all?" "We were wondering, since we are new here, in the city, if you could suggest some good places to get something to eat."

"Are y'all looking for a place just to eat, or do y'all want to go someplace with music, food and drinks?" "Ideally all three," Jana chips in, laughing. "Well, in that case, there's a place on Peachtree Street that should offer all that you are looking for. It's a place called the Ex Lounge." The girls get excited about the Ex Lounge after getting the information that they needed.

The property manager gives them the directions to the place and the girls all load up in Sinclair's car and make their way to the lounge. "I can't believe that we are here!" exclaims Jana. Amazed by the huge building and lights on their way downtown, Jana is excited to see so many fast cars that pass by. "Now, this is my kind of place!" "What are you talking about?" asks Christy. "Just look at all the young people out here driving these nice cars. I bet it's would be nice to be in their shoes."

The girls continue on their way to the Ex Lounge still hearing Jana's excited chatter coming from the backseat. "Jana, you are a little too excited about material things," notes Christy. "There's no telling what those young people you are seeing are doing to be in those fly rides," she adds. "I don't care because, whatever they are doing, they are doing it big. I need to find out what exactly they are doing so I can do it with them. I am not trying to live my life working for anybody. I want to be my own boss and do what I want to do when I want to do it."

"We are not suggesting that you can't be your own boss; all we are saying is that you don't want to do something stupid to get what you want," say Sinclair. "The way I feel now is that I will do anything to be on top and not have to worry about answering to anybody." Stunned by what Jana is saying, the girls finally locate the Ex Lounge, find a parking space and enter the restaurant.

"Wow, this place is really nice!" says Sinclair. "I can get used to a place like this," adds Jana. Sinclair and Christy are still amazed at how open Jana has become in just a short time of being in Atlanta. The hostess approaches the ladies with a menu and asks them if they would like to sit at the bar or a get a table for three. They all agree to sit at the table. As the girls are taken to their table, Sinclair asks Christy to accompany her to the ladies room.

Jana quickly grabs the drinks menu to order a drink. "What will y'all like to have to drink?" asks the hostess. Looking over the menu, Jana replies, "I would like to have a Long Island." "Do you know what your friends would like?" "They can order when they return," she replies. "This is really a nice place," she notes to herself as the hostess departs with her order.

Looking around the lounge, Jana notices that many handsome men are staring at her from the bar. She smiles as if she is a kid in a candy store. Not only is she noticing the guys checking her out, but she also notes their watches, necklaces, and earrings they are wearing. "They must be some real ballers," she whispers to herself. She also notices a group of women, wearing high heels, tight fitted skirts, and designer bags, sitting on the other side of the lounge.

"Strippers," she says to herself. "But I can't lie, those hoes are doing it big over there," she adds. The waitress comes back with her Long Island and checks again with Jana to see if her friends would want a drink. "Those bitches will be back soon," she retorts, rather rudely.

Meanwhile, in the ladies' room, Sinclair and Christy are discussing a little change that they see in Jana. "What do you think she is up to?" asks Sinclair. "I mean, we both know her, but you, Christy, know her a little better than me." "I remember, back in school, how she would be talking about how ready she was to come to Atlanta, and how things were going to be different." "I wonder what she has up her sleeve. I think that all this stuff that happened back home has taken a toll on her," Sinclair notes.

"With being raped and having that abortion, I think she is trying to overcome the pain and shock by acting out," Christy suggests. "When we went back to school, she would wake up in the middle of the night, crying, as if she wanted to give up." "I think she really took that situation hard and is now trying to hide it inside," says Sinclair. "We just have to watch her and make sure that she doesn't do anything stupid." "Well, let's hurry back and get to our table and make sure she hadn't already started doing something stupid," Sinclair urges.

The girls laugh and head back to their table to sit down with Jana, noting on their arrival that Jana has already started drinking. "What y'all bitches were up to in the bathroom?" she asks. "What do you mean? We did what one is supposed to do in the bathroom," objects Christy. "Don't get smart, bitch!" "Why am I a bitch all of a sudden?" "I'm just saying that y'all had to be talking about me in there." "Why do you think that?" says Sinclair.

"Because y'all bitches didn't invite me to come join y'all!" "We assumed that you wanted to stay out here and admire the scenery," says Sinclair. "Whatever, bitches!" she says rather loudly, causing some customers to look in their direction. "What are you drinking?" asks Christy. "A Long Island," she responds. "You have finished that already." "Yes and am now about to order another one," she retorts stubbornly.

The waitress comes back over to the table to take Sinclair's and Christy's orders. "What would you ladies be having?" "Please bring me a glass of water," says Sinclair. "I would like a sweet tea," adds Christy. "And for me, another Long Island!" Jana shouts. Everybody stares at Jana, noticing that the first drink she had has already had an effect on her. "Jana, you don't think one is enough?" asks Sinclair with concern.

"I mean, those Long Island are very strong." "You don't have to prove a point," adds Christy. "I'm not trying to prove anything; I'm just trying to enjoy myself." "You can enjoy yourself without drinking so much." "Look, remember what I told y'all the last time we were out, that I am grown and I can take care of myself?" "Yes, we remember," says Sinclair. "Well, I meant that and I will be just fine." "Ok, and you remember what happened last time you got yourself really drunk too Jana?" objects Sinclair. With that being said, Jana stares down Sinclair with anger in her eyes, shocked that she would bring something like that up in her face. "Excuse me," she says, as she gets up from the table and leaves for the restroom.

"You didn't have to say that," Christy reprimands Sinclair. "She needed to hear the truth," she responds. "I just don't want to go through anything like we did back home. We are here in Atlanta to make a clean start. If we were going to do the same things, we could have just stayed back at home." "You are right," Christy agrees. "Let me go and check on her in the restroom," she adds.

As Christy gets up from the table and goes to the restroom to find Jana, Sinclair begins to feel very sorry for what she just said. While in the restroom, Christy sees Jana crying. "She didn't mean it like it sounded, you know," says Christy. "Look, both of y'all have been through a lot in the past couple of months and it's hard. Still, you have to overcome that, be strong and move on." "It just hurts so badly to think about what I've been through. So, when I have those thoughts, I try to drink to relax," says Jana.

"You know that you cannot drink your problems away. You can't solve any issues that way. The best thing for you to do is talk with me or Sinclair if you want to get over something. We are here for you if you ever need to talk about something. I promise you that she didn't mean what she said. What we need to do is go back to our table and enjoy the rest of this evening in the city we call our new home and celebrate the new beginning. Remember what we said when we left Baltimore—a new city, a new home, and a new life."

Jana and Christy are back at the table to join Sinclair. "Is everything ok?" "Yes," says Jana. "I want to say that I am sorry for saying what I did and that I really did not wish to offend you." "I know you meant it in a good way. We are friends to the end, like Chucky," says Jana. They are interrupted by the waitress, who comes back to the table with a bottle of Moet that a gentleman from the bar had sent over.

"Oh hell, no!" yells Sinclair. "I remember this scene. With no disrespect, please inform the gentleman that sent this bottle of Moet over here that we are ok and that we cannot accept it," she tells the waitress. With a smile, the waitress removes the Moet and delivers it, and the message behind it, to the gentleman. "Now, that was way to strange!" says Christy. "There was no way we were going back down that road again," adds Jana.

Just in that short period of time, the girls could reflect on the night at the Pool Hall and everything that had taken place. "I do not ever want to see another bottle of Moet in my life," says Sinclair. "And if I never see one myself again, I would be very happy," says Christy. "That was scary," adds Jana.

The girls regroup and take a deep breath, realizing the implications of what had just happened. Jana takes a drink from her Long Island, puts her hand on her chin, shaking her head in disbelief. "Ok, time to order now," she says, gesturing to the waitress, who comes back to the table to take their food orders. "What was that all about?" she asks.

"It's a long story, but trust that we won't be accepting anybody's drink offers anymore," says Sinclair. "He was pretty shocked that you ladies returned his offer," the waitress notes, referring to the gentleman at the bar. "We just had our fair share of accepting drinks from guys and it just wasn't a god experience," says Jana. The waitress, still with a puzzled look on her face, takes their orders. "What would you like?" she asks.

"I would like the chicken pasta with a side salad," says Sinclair. "My choice is the shrimp pasta and a garden salad," says Christy. "I would like the lasagna and a garden salad," adds Jana. With that, the waitress leaves the table and the girls resume their conversation. "Look, the guy is looking at us," says Christy. "I don't know why he is looking over here; as we didn't accept his drink, he should just get over it and move on," adds Sinclair.

"That was kind of mean, now that I think about it," Jana objects. "We could have just taken it and not drink it, just to make him feel good." "That would just be leading him on," says Christy. "I have no problem with telling a guy 'no', and if it hurts their feelings, then so be it," Sinclair adds. "Maybe that's where we are different, because I don't like to be mean to anybody trying to be nice to me," Jana observes. "But sometimes if you have been through something that wasn't good for you, it's ok to turn it down," Christy joins in.

About forty-five minutes later, the girls are just about fin-ished with their meals. Suddenly, they notice that the guy who offered them the bottle of Moet is headed towards their table. "Look, he is coming over here!" Christy whispers. Sinclair looks at the guy coming towards them. "I hate to be mean, but I will, if he doesn't get the hint," she says. "We don't have to be rude to his, he did nothing to deserve it," objects Jana.

Arriving at their table, the guy addressed the girls, "How you ladies are doing? My name is Jerome. And you are?" he says with a smile. "I'm Sinclair." "I'm Christy." "I'm Jana."— they say respectively. "I got a little offended to see that my offer was returned." "We appreciate your generous offer, but we're ok," Sinclair is the first to respond. "We just had some bad experiences from accepting offers like that in the past," says Christy. "It just brought up many memories that we didn't want to think about," adds Jana.

"I can respect that. Are you ladies from here?" "Actually no; we moved here today," says Jana. "From where?" he asks. "Baltimore." "Well let me become the first to say 'welcome to Atlanta'." "Hey, we respect your braveness to come over here to introduce yourself, but we are enjoying this evening amongst ourselves and we would like to continue that," says Sinclair.

With that being said, Jerome pulls out a business card and hands it to Jana. "If you ladies ever need any information about what's happening in the city, feel free to call me," he says and walks off. "That was so mean of you girls. He was just being nice," says Jana.

After finishing up their meals and drinks, the girls pay their tab and leave the Ex Lounge. "One down and a thousand more to go," jokes Sinclair, referring to the many more places to go in Atlanta. "I hope we can remember how to get back to the apartment," notes Christy. "I think that I remember," says Jana. The girls get back onto the expressway, driving under the speed limit to avoid unwelcome attention of the local police, trying to remember how to get back home.

"I think that we should take 75 north; to 285 south to get to Cobb Parkway," says Sinclair. With no knowledge of how to get back to the apartment, Christy grabs the apartment guide to get the directions. "Yes you were right Sinclair; we are going in the right direction." "Jana, are you alright?" asks Christy. With no response from Jana, Christy turns to look in the back seat. She sees Jana out cold, asleep in the back seat of the car.

"I guess those Long Islands had a pretty good effect on Ms. Jana. This girl is out cold," Christy notes. "From all this moving, and not to mention how much we just ate, I am so ready to get in the bed," adds Sinclair. "Tomorrow is Sunday and I promised my grandma that I was going to find a church to attend. Speaking of my grandma, I forgot to call her and let her know that we made it safely." "I need to call my mother as well." With that, Sinclair proceeds to their destination.

Back in her apartment, Sinclair gets her cell phone to call Grandma. "Did y'all make it ok?" asks Grandma. "Yes ma'm." "So how is it so far?" "Well, we spent most of the day unloading and unpacking, so we really didn't have much time to do anything else," says Sinclair. "Where is Tiffany?" "Asleep. That girl played so much today, that when she came into the house, she went straight to bed." "I guess, I will talk with her tomorrow then."

"Did Jana and Christy get themselves situated in their apartments yet?" "We are all in the same situation. By tomorrow or the next day we should be fully unpacked and settled in our new homes." "When you get a chance, I need you to find a church that you will call home from now on and continue to call on the Lord for guidance." "I was just saying to Christy that I needed to do that." "That's good to hear." "Well Grandma, give Tiffany a kiss for me and tell Uncle Pete that I said 'hello' and that we made it safely to our new home."

"You know how Uncle Pete gets when he hasn't heard from me in a while," Sinclair adds with a smile. "I sure will do that baby, and call me from time to time, so that we can know how you are doing," says Grandma. "I promise to call you every other day and check in with y'all, Grandma." Sinclair and Grandma finish up their conversation and get off the phone. Sinclair then showers and prepares for bed. "I will deal with you boxes tomorrow," she says, turning to the pile of unopened packages, and falls asleep.

The next day comes and Sinclair awakes from her sleep. "Man, it's Sunday and I need to start unpacking these boxes," she says to herself. "This is going to take all day." As she starts to unpack, she gets a call on her cell phone. "Who would be calling this early in the morning?" She wonders, grabbing her phone. Once she sees that the call is from Derrick, she smiles and answers the call.

"Hello, or shall I say good morning?" Derrick greets her warmly. "What are you doing, calling me early in the morning?" "I thought that I would wake you up and put a smile on your face." "You did, and I needed that." "So what's going on in Baltimore?" "Baltimore," she responds. "We are now in Atlanta." "What?" he asks, clearly in shock. "You heard me. We are in Atlanta now." "That's great. Why didn't you just tell me that earlier?" he asks, clearly confused. "Well, have you gotten situated?" "I'm in the process of doing that now."

"I have so many boxes that I have to unpack and I don't know if I will get them all done today." "I would come over there and help you, but you would have to pay me a hundred dollars an hour," he says, laughing. "Whatever," she responds playfully. "I don't mind helping. If you like, I could come over there and help you unpack your boxes, if you are ok with that." "Feel free," she says, giving Derrick the address.

An hour later, Derrick is knocking at Sinclair's door. "It's about time you made it," she says jokingly. "Damn, what did you not bring? You have in here everything except the kitchen sink," he says. "Don't complain, just unpack." "Where should I begin?" "Start with the large boxes, because they have the dishes and the pots and pans."

Sinclair and Derrick start unpacking, going through each box pretty quickly. He stumbles up on a shoe box that contains Sinclair's photos. He pulls out one particular photo that catches his eyes. "Who is this gorgeous lady?" Sinclair walks over to see the photo he is referring too and noticing whom it is of, she grabs the photo. "That's a picture of my mother when she was in her twenties. I think she was twenty two. I was two months old then." "You look a lot like your mother.

Where is she now?" "My mom passed away when I was fifteen years old."

"I am so sorry to hear that." Sinclair goes on tell him her mother's situation and all what she knew of her mother, including what her grandmother told her. Derrick listens, paying close attention to every detail. "I know that it has been hard for you lately, but I just want to tell you that you are a strong woman and everything is going to be fine now that you here in Atlanta." Sinclair stares at him with a smile and gives him a hug.

Derrick holds her tight, looking into her eyes. As she sees the passion in his eyes, she comes even closer towards him. "I will never hurt you," he says. "I really want us to get to know each other and explore this city together," he adds. "I just don't want to rush anything," she says. "You can take as much time as you need, but know that I am here for you."

Reassured by those words, Sinclair feels very comfortable in his arms. He puts his finger under her chin and raises it gently. As he stares at her soft lips, the desire to kiss them is overpowering. She notices that look in his eyes and hints to him that she wants his lips on hers. He moves forward and kisses them passionately. The kiss gets them both heated and he carries her in his arms into her bedroom; laying her gently across the bed, still kissing her passionately.

He removes his shirt, before taking her white tank top off. He starts kissing her on her neck and moves slowly to her breasts. As he starts caressing them gently and softly with his warm lips, she begins to moan, rubbing her fingers through his hair, wanting more. He moves down to her belly button and begins to caress it slowly with his tongue. He then removes her pajamas, leaving her naked.

Fuelled by his desire for her, he gets off the bed to remove the rest of his clothes. Now naked, he gets back on the bed and begins to suck on her entire body from head to toe. Enjoying his caresses with her eyes closed, her body begins to shake nervously. He continues exciting her even more. Finally, he opens her legs and begins to stroke her clitoris. Sinclair is now hot and wet from Derrick's foreplay.

He gets a condom, puts it on and enters her vagina. Sinclair moans, welcoming his penis inside her. "Don't hurt me," she says. "I won't," he responds. With his every stroke, come passionate moans from Sinclair. The two take every position that they can think of before finally reaching orgasm. Afterwards, Sinclair falls asleep in his arms, very satisfied.

"What now?" he asks. "What does this mean? Was this just sex or do we continue and try to be together now?" "I think we can try and see where this goes. I mean, I want to be able to trust you before committing to a relationship. With you playing football and everything, I hope that you really want to be with me." "I meant every word that came out of my mouth. Girls come with the territory, because I play football, but I don't want them, I want you."

"I just want you to know that, if you hurt me once, I will be done with you, no matter what." "I will never hurt you and all I want you to do is trust me." "I will trust you until you give me a reason not to." Later that night, Sinclair awakens from her nap and goes to the bathroom to take a shower.

"Can I join you?" "I think you had enough for the day." "I can never get enough of you." "I bet that you can't," she responds. While she is taking her shower, Derrick hears a knock at the door. "Someone is at your door," he yells to Sinclair. "It might be Christy or Jana. Answer it for me." He goes to answer the door with his shirt still off and his pants unbuckled. He looks through the peek hole and, after seeing Christy standing at the door, he lets her in.

"Well, hello stranger!" she greets his in surprise. "How have you been?" she asks. "I've been doing fine." Christy catches a glimpse of his nice body, noticing that he is checking out her ass in those short tight fitted shorts she has on. "Being a football player and everything, I bet you have to work out every day," she comments playfully with a seductive look on her face.

"Not every day, but I try to get a few days in during the week." "I think I can use a little exercise myself." "You look good to me," he says with a devilish look in his eyes. "Maybe one day you can be my fitness trainer." "Who knows, maybe," he says. They both stare at each other with a smile on their face. "Who is it?" asks Sinclair from the back room. "It's only me, trick," Christy shouts out jokingly. "I see that you got your boxes unpacked and shit." "Thanks to Derrick, as he came to help me get them unpacked."

"I see that he helped you with something else too," Christy notes, laughing. "Mind your own business." "Y'all crazy,"

Derrick joins in. "I am going to let y'all girls kick it and I'm going to head back to the crib. I will call you later," he says to Sinclair. "Take care, Christy," he turns to Christy. "Bye," she responds.

Finally alone, Christy follows Sinclair in the backroom so she could finish getting dressed. "So y'all did it, didn't y'all?" "You are so nosey!" "I smell it in the air, that's why I am asking." "Maybe, maybe not." "So how was it to do it with a football player?" "No different from doing it with a basketball player. But I'm not going to lie girl, his penis was huge!" she says, smiling. "He wore me out, girl."

"Damn girl, he put your ass to sleep." "I haven't done it in almost three months, so I knew it was going to be a little uncomfortable for me." "So are y'all going to be a couple now?" "We are going to take it slowly and just get to know each other a little better." "Looks to me that y'all have gotten to know each other a lot!" Christy notes with a cheeky smile. "Girl, when he came to that door with his shirt off, I was tempted to jump on him myself."

"You just make sure you don't get curious and mess with my man," says Sinclair jokingly. "So he's your man now?" "Not at the moment, but he will be. I already have a challenge on my hand with him being a football player, trying to keep the groupies off him. I don't need to look over my shoulders to see my best friend after him too." "Trust me, I don't want your man." "Enough of this crazy talk, where is Jana?" asks Sinclair, keen to change the rather uncomfortable subject.

"I tried calling her cell phone, but she didn't answer," says Christy. "We should go to her apartment and check on her," suggests Sinclair. Soon they are knocking at Jana's door, but she doesn't answer. They knock several times, but still no answer. They both begin to get a little concerned about Jana, since she hasn't been answering her phone or the door.

"I see her car is still here, but why isn't she picking up her cell phone or answering the door?" wonders Sinclair, not really concerned. "I hope that girl hasn't done anything stupid to herself," says Christy. The girls' knocks begin to get louder and louder, to the point where the next door neighbor can hear them. "I saw your girl leaving early this morning with some dude," says the neighbor. "Do you know what kind of car they were in?" asks Sinclair.

"They were in a black Tahoe." "Ok, thank you." They try to call Jana again, but fail to get an answer. "Look, I'm tired of that girl doing stupid shit," says Christy. "I hate to give up on her, but she needs to get it together," agrees Sinclair. "Let's just go back to my apartment and wait for her," she suggests.

Just as they are leaving, they see a black Tahoe pulling around the corner. As it halts to a stop, they see Jana getting out. Sinclair and Christy walk towards her. "What the hell are you doing?" yells Sinclair. "We were worried sick about you," adds Christy. "Do y'all remember Jerome from the Ex Lounge? Well, we went to have brunch together, that's all." "You can't be leaving with strangers and not let anyone know where you are going," objects Sinclair. "Look, you're not my mother, so stop treating me as if you were. I am so sick of y'all trying to tell me what to do and shit, as if I'm some little girl. I can take care of myself and I suggest y'all do the same," she says angrily.

"And for your information, Jerome is cool. We have been talking every since I came home last night." "Look if you don't want us to worry about you then we won't," retorts Sinclair. "From this day forward, Jana will do what Jana wants to do," adds Christy. After the heated exchange, Jana walks off, enters her apartment and slams the door.

"Look we just need to give her space and let her learn from her own mistakes," says Sinclair. "Let's just hope that she doesn't make many to where she can't get out of them herself," adds Christy. "I'm not going to let this gorgeous day go by worrying about Jana. As far as I'm concerned, she is on her own, free to do whatever she wants to do," says Sinclair.

CHAPTER 7

"What are we going to do about Jana?" asks Sinclair. "I mean, she's clearly going through a lot but it's like she is scared to seek help." "We just have to give her some time and maybe she will come around and want to talk about whatever she is going through," says Christy. After having a long discussion about Jana, Christy and Sinclair decide to go and get familiar with the city.

"It's a little after 1 o'clock, and before it gets too late, I think we need to go and see what the city has to offer," Sinclair suggests. They get into Sinclair's car and head into the city. In the meantime, Jana is back at her apartment, still angry from the argument she had with Sinclair and Christy. She picks up the phone to call the girls, keen to apologize for her behavior earlier.

"It's Jana," says Sinclair looking at her phone. "I wonder what she wants," says Christy. Sinclair answers her cell phone. "Hello Jana, what's up?" "I just want to apologize for my actions earlier today." "Jana, all we want is for you to make better decisions. We all know that you have been through a lot and so have we, but you have to let the past be the past, learn from that and move on."

After hearing Sinclair say that, Jana starts to sob on the other side of the line. "Why are you crying, Jana?" "I just feel that I'm losing it. It's hard not to think about what happened a couple months ago, but I can't help it," cries Jana. "I've had nightmares about that night I was raped and it scares me so much."

"I never been in that situation, but I can imagine how horribly you must feel," Sinclair notes, shaking her head in sorrow for Jana. "Christy and I are on our way to tour the city and when we get back we will come over and talk some more with you." Jana agrees and tells her that she is just going to take a nap until they get back to the apartment. "She is really taking it hard," says Sinclair, as she hangs up.

"Jana and I never really had that father figure we could look up to, to help us with situations like the one Jana is going through." "True, but friends can help is difficult times too. We just need to monitor her behavior and make sure that she remains strong until she can get over her depression," says Christy. Still discussing Jana's emotional breakdown, the girls continue on their journey to see what the city has to offer.

There are so many fascinating things that they can see. They pass the newly created Centennial Park, the legendary Gladys Night Chicken and Waffles, the World of Coca Cola, and they even visit Dr. Martin Luther King Jr.'s monument. After such an amazing day out, they decide that it is time to head back to the apartment to check on Jana.

"Now that was a tour for the ages!" exclaims Christy. "I can't believe that we were able to ride through downtown and not get lost," adds Sinclair. "If we do this for a few more weeks, we should get to know the city pretty quickly," she notes. Back at the apartment, Jana is still feeling very depressed. She is sitting on the sofa, drinking a glass of wine, trying to dull her pain.

She picks up the phone to call Jerome. "Hey gorgeous, what's going on?" he greets her. "I feel as if the walls are closing in on me." "Why do you say that?" Jana begins to get really comfortable with Jerome and confides in him. "I have been through so much these past couple of months." "You can tell me anything, so spill your guts," he offers, sounding sincere.

"Remember how, when we met you yesterday at the Ex Lounge and you sent over that bottle of Moet, we refused it?" "Yes, I remember." "My depression is related to the reason behind us not accepting your generous offer. Back in Baltimore, we met a few guys that sent over a bottle of Moet and, after that, the night got a little bizarre." Listening to Jana, Jerome seems a little curious to know just what Jana is talking about.

Jana continues telling him what happened that night at the Pool Hall. "After we had drinks and the night was almost ending, a huge fight broke out between Sinclair's boyfriend Kenneth and her new friend Derrick." "What else happened?" he asks. "I was taken by this guy named Chris who ended up killing Kenneth that night. That same night, Chris had spiked my drink and took me away to his place in D.C."

"What happened when you got to his place?" "He raped me," she says, crying. "Damn, I'm sorry to hear that. Guys that do that to someone need to be put in jail for good," he notes sympathetically. "Well, there is more." After a few seconds of silence, Jana continues with her story. "Following the rape, I found out that getting was pregnant," she says, still crying, as the painful memories of that night run through her mind.

She continues to tell Jerome about what ended up happening to Chris after everything went down. "After a few weeks on the run, Chris was apprehended by the police, as he came to see me at my place. He was convicted of first degree murder and rape and was sentenced to life in prison without parole." "So, I guess you decided to get an abortion?" asks Jerome. "I could not have a baby with a man that did that to me. I knew in my mind that I was going to get an abortion as soon as I found out."

"I understand now why y'all would turn down any drink that a man offered y'all at a club." "So, I hope that now you realize that it was no knock against you; we just didn't want to remember that night and what we went through afterwards. Although my friend Sinclair was being a little rude, I thought that you were cool, which is why I called you." "Well, that's good to know, and I hope we can get to know each other a little more," says Jerome. "We'll see," she responds.

Soon, Sinclair and Christy arrive at Jana apartment and she ends her conversation with Jerome to open the door for her friends. "Why are you sitting in the dark?" asks Sinclair. "And you are drinking; what's wrong now?" says Christy. "I just wanted to relax, listen to some music and have a drink," Jana explains. "What is wrong with that?" she adds. "I just find it strange for you to be sitting in the dark by yourself, drinking an entire bottle of wine," objects Sinclair.

"Look, if you came over here to judge me, then you can do me a favor and leave." "Look, Jana, we are here to help you and finish what we were talking about earlier." Sinclair and Christy take a seat and accept a glass of wine offered by Jana. "I think my biggest problem is not having the baby," says Jana. "Even though the way the pregnancy happened, that may have been the only time that I could have gotten pregnant."

"Don't say that," says Christy. "You did the right thing by not having that baby," she adds. "Sinclair surly thought differently," Jana notes, turning to Sinclair, who is staring at her with a confused expression. "Let me clear up what I said, so that you can understand me better. I said that, if that were me, I would have kept the baby, but you and I are two different people," she shouts. "Apparently, you did the right thing, because the way that you are acting now shows that you can't handle it. With that being said, I think I need to leave." Sinclair grabs her bag and leaves Jana's apartment very upset.

After Sinclair leaves, Christy tries to talk with Jana. "Both of y'all are going through a lot. She is hurting just as much as you are. Still, this was supposed to be a positive move. We are here in this new city and we need to stick together and be strong." "You cannot even start to imagine what I'm feeling inside," says Jana. "It hurts like hell and I all I can do is try to drink my problems away."

"That's not good and you know that turning to drink every time you get depressed will only make matters worse." "I just want this pain to go away." "It will eventually, but you have to give it some time." "Sometimes I feel like giving up and have no desire to live," Jana says with a blank look on her face. Christy stares at Jana, surprised to hear her friend speak so negatively. "Are you saying what I think you are?" "Sometimes, I just feel like this is all life will ever offer to me, and if so, life sucks."

"You can't think like that, because one thing you don't want to do is take your own life. You have to know that you will be hurting a lot of people that love you if you did that. Life is a challenge, but you have to make the best of it and try to remain positive. Just promise me as your best friend that you will be strong and not do anything stupid," says Christy. Jana, the blank look still on her face, promises to Christy that she would not harm herself. They give each other a hug and Christy leaves Jana's apartment.

It's Monday, two days after the girls moved to Atlanta. Sinclair has to meet with her boss today to get the itinerary for her marketing job that she will be starting next week. Christy begins her new job at the bank on Wednesday, where she is appointed as a Branch Manager, and Jana is to report to her job on Tuesday at the phone company as a Public Relations Director.

As Sinclair is leaving her apartment, she runs into Christy. "How did the conversation turn out last night?" "Sinclair, it's more serious than you think." "What do you mean 'more serious'?" "Well, after you left, we started talking about Jana's situation more in depth; as we were talking she was fading in and out of a daze. I assumed that it was because of the wine we were drinking, but it wasn't that." "What was it then?"

"I think that she wants to commit suicide or something. She started talking about how life isn't fair and how she wants to give up." "What else did she say?" "Everything was pretty much about her saying that she wanted to give up on life. I made her promise me that she wouldn't do anything to hurt herself and she agreed that she wouldn't." "How many times has Jana made a promise to either you or me and ended up doing the opposite?" objects Sinclair, now truly concerned for her friend's wellbeing. "Well, I hope that she is really sincere about what she says. I am going to pray tonight that she remains strong and gains a more positive outlook on life," says Sinclair. "I will do the same," notes Christy and the two friends part.

After the talk with Christy, Sinclair gets into her car with a concerned look on her face. She drives off to meet up with her boss. Christy rushes off to run some errands of her own. "I guess I will check on Jana to see if she is feeling a little better," she says to herself. She gets her cell phone and calls Jana, but Jana does not answer. She calls several more times, but still there's no answer from Jana. "Maybe she is still asleep," she tries to reassure herself.

Unable to stop worrying, knowing that there is a possibility that Jana could harm herself, Christy somehow still manages to continue running her errands. Later that evening,

Sinclair is back from her appointment with her boss and Christy is at home too. After asking each other about their day, they decide to go over and check on Jana. When they arrive to her door they run into her next door neighbor.

"Hello ladies," he says. "Y'all need to check on your girl." "Why, what happened?" they asks. "Your girl was out in the parking lot earlier today, pacing back and forth for no apparent reason." He goes on to say that Jana had no shoes on and was only wearing a white tank top and some boy shorts. "I think the girl has lost it," he says in a sarcastic way. "Thank you for the information," Sinclair responds, as the girls rush to the door to check on Jana. Despite their knocks and shouts, there is no answer from inside the apartment.

"Her car is still in the same spot," says Christy. "Let me call her cell phone again." She does, but gets no answer. They get really concerned now. After hearing what the neighbor said, combined with Jana not responding, they do the best thing they can think off—contact the leasing office.

"We have a situation with our friend," says Sinclair to the property manager. "What seems to be the problem?" "We believe that our friend is locked inside her apartment and is harmed. Could y'all hurry and come and open her door, so that we can see if our friend is inside. Please hurry, please." Sinclair gets off the phone with the property manager and waits impatiently until someone from the leasing office comes to open Jana's apartment door.

About five minutes later, the maintenance man comes to open the door. "It took you long enough!" snorts Christy. "I just got the page to come open the door and I came as soon as I could, given that the apartment is located way in the back," he says. The man opens the door and Sinclair and Christy run in to find Jana. They look in the bedroom, only to find it empty. They then go into the bathroom, but the door is locked. "How do we get in?" Christy asks to the maintenance man in alarm. They knock on the door, but receive no answer from Jana. The maintenance man burst the door open to see Jana lying in the full bathtub, with pills spilled all over the floor.

They scream out Jana's name over and over; tears coming from their eyes. "No, no, no!" screams Sinclair in despair. "Jana, wake up!" they shout trying to revive her. The maintenance man gets his cell phone out and dials 911. "We have a young lady that appears to have taken an overdose of medication pills and we need assistance here quickly," he says. He gives the operator the information that they need to get to the apartment as quickly as possible. Jana is completely out.

Sinclair and Christy remove Jana from the tub and cover her with some towels. Still crying and screaming her name, they try really hard to get Jana to wake up. Still there is no response from Jana. Ten minutes later, the ambulance is pulling into the apartment complex, sirens blazing. The paramedics rush up the stairs into the apartment where Jana is lying down.

"Back up please so we can help her to respond," says the EMS. "She has no pulse," someone yells. "We need to get her breathing again," another one observes. They put an oxygen mask over her face and proceed to do CPR on Jana. Sinclair and Christy are crying nervously, hoping that their friend can still be helped. The paramedics get the defibrillator and begin to put it to Jana's chest.

"Clear," they say, pressing the pads on her chest, but still no response. "Clear," they do it again and still no response. "Let's do it one more time," they say. "Clear; we have a pulse," they say. Jana opens her eyes but looks really drugged up from all the meds she has taken. "We have to get her to the hospital quickly," the EMS notes. They put Jana on a stretcher and take her into the ambulance, to take her to the emergency room. Sinclair and Christy get into their car and follow behind.

The two worried friends rush to the hospital, desperate to know how Jana is doing, hoping that she is safely in the ICU for further evaluation. "I can't believe Jana tried to take her life," says Sinclair. "I am shocked myself," adds Christy. "All this time, we were thinking that this was something that she could get through. Now, we come to find out that she was taking it harder than we could have imagined," says Sinclair.

They enter the hospital and rush to the front desk to see where Jana has been taken. "Excuse me," Christy greets the nurse at the desk. "How may I help you?" the nurse responds. "Could you tell us where they have taken a patient by the name of Jana Gay?" The nurse gets her chart out to look up the name that Christy has given her. "She is in ICU room number 301," she replies and the two friends rush off.

They are stopped by the nurse, who advises them that only family members are allowed to visit Jana at the moment. "Are y'all related to the patient?" she asks. "We are her closest friends and we all grew up together," Sinclair replies. "As I said before, if you are not family, then you are going to have to wait to see your friend."

Sinclair and Christy get really irritated. "We are the only family she has here and we need to find out if she is doing ok!" Sinclair shouts, losing her patience. After some back and forth lashes between them, Christy grabs Sinclair and tells her to calm down, suggesting that they wait in the visitor's room until further notice. The nurse tells then that she will keep them updated on Jana's situation.

After a seemingly endless wait in the visiting room, the doctor comes out to meet with Sinclair and Christy and give them an update on Jana's situation. "Hello ladies." "How is our friend doing?" asks Sinclair, unable to wait any longer for the news on Jana. "Is she going to be ok?" Christy interrupts. "Right now, she is in stable condition. It seems to me that your friend had a history of drug abuse," he says. "Why would you say that?" asks Sinclair. "Well, we found amphetamines in her blood."

"You mean that she has been using speed?" Christy asks, clearly astonished. "I'm afraid so; amphetamines are stimulants that accelerate functions in the brain and the body. These drugs hit users with a fast high, making them feel powerful, alert, and energized. Have you two noticed anything unusual about your friend before this happened?" "She seems to have been very depressed lately from an incident that happened several months ago," says Sinclair. "We were aware of the issue and it was not surprising that a rather traumatic situation she went through had an effect on her," she adds. "She started drinking a lot and seems to always want to stay high for some reason," adds Christy. "She would sometimes have mood swings."

"Amphetamines are psychologically addictive. The users who tried to stop reported that they had experienced various mood problems, such as aggression, anxiety, and intense craving for the drugs. Prolonged use may cause hallucinations and intense paranoia," the doctor explains. "Is she going to be ok?" asks Sinclair. "While she is here, we are going to make sure that she is looked after," the doctor reassures her. "She is going to need plenty of rest and when she wakes up, we are going to give her further tests to make sure she has a normal function throughout her body." He adds.

Sinclair and Christy thank the doctor for the information that he provided, feeling a little better, knowing that their friend will survive another scary and frightening situation. "We have to get her some help fast," says Sinclair. "This is not what we expected to happen." "This move to Atlanta was to be a new start and a welcome change from what we been through in the past. We cannot have any more drama now," says Christy. "I have to call my grandma and let her know what is going on," adds Sinclair.

While waiting in the emergency room, Sinclair gets her cell phone out to call her grandma. "Hey Grandma," she greets her. From the tone in her voice, Grandma knows that something is wrong, and asks Sinclair, "What's wrong?" "It's Jana." "What's wrong with Jana?" "They had to take her to the hospital because she tried to commit suicide." "Suicide?" shouts Grandma. "Why would she do a thing like that?" "Apparently, Jana has a problem with drugs that we didn't know about. The doctor did some tests and found out that she has been using drugs for quite some time now." "Is she going to be ok?" "Yes ma'm. She is resting now and when she awakens, we will be allowed to go and see her. Grandma, what are we going to do with her?"

"We want to help her, but what if she doesn't want to be helped?" "When you get the opportunity to talk to her, find out if she wants help. Explain to her that she is not only hurting herself, but she is hurting the people that love her as well." "What if that doesn't work Grandma? What do we do then?" "If that doesn't work, then just leave it in God's hands and hope for the best. I mean, Jana is grown woman, and if she doesn't want to be helped, then you can't force her to accept your offer. There is only so much that you can do to try and help someone."

"You are right, Grandma. I am going to do everything in my power to make sure that Jana gets the help that she needs. I am not going to give up unless she pushes me completely away." "You must also remember, Sinclair, that at the end of the day, you make sure you are taking care of yourself. Everybody has problems, but if you don't correct your problems, then you can't really help other people with their problem."

After about thirty minutes on the phone with her grandma, Sinclair begins to feel much better than before. Grandma sends her best wishes and prayers out to Jana and reminds Sinclair that prayer is power, and if she wants answers, she should refer to God and the Bible to help her get through what she needs to get through. Sinclair tells her grandma how much she loves her and reminds her to tell Tiffany 'hello'. She ends the call with a goodbye.

Still waiting in the visitor's room, Sinclair and Christy are informed to come back tomorrow to see their friend. They are told that Jana is going to need the rest of the day to sleep and get the rest she really needs. After agreeing with the nurse, they grab their belongings and go home. "I am very surprised to know that Jana had been using drugs before the incident," Christy notes on the way out. "That shocked me too," Sinclair agrees. "Remember when her next door neighbor said that she was pacing back and forth in the parking lot? We should have known that something was wrong then," she adds, feeling guilty for not paying more attention to Jana.

"It was the effects of the drugs that made her act that way," says Christy. "Talking with my grandma made me feel a little better," Sinclair changes the subject. "What did she say?" "She just said to try and get Jana some help as much as we can and hope that she wants the help." "What if she doesn't want our help? You know how stubborn she can be, then what we do?" "Well, as Grandma said, if a grown person doesn't want to be helped, then you can't help them."

"I mean, we are going to do as much as we can to help her and hope that she accepts the help, but if she doesn't, then we just wash our hands clean and let Jana do what Jana wants to do," Sinclair adds with renewed determination. "We grew up together and we have been close since we were kids. I love her with all my heart, but I'm with you on that, Sinclair. If we try to help her and she refuses the help, she will be on her own," Christy agrees. With that, the girls head home from the hospital.

The next day, before they go back to the hospital to visit Jana, they decide to find the help that Jana is going to need. They begin their search around the city that morning to find a therapist that Jana could talk to. They meet Dr. Samantha Cain, a specialist in mental health issues. "Hello my name is Sinclair and this is my friend Christy." "How can I help you ladies?" The girls enter the office take a seat and begin to talk with Dr. Cain.

"We have a friend that needs help." "What seems to be her problem?" Sinclair begins to rub her hands together, suddenly hesitant to tell the therapist what she needs to know about Jana. Sensing her uneasiness, Christy interrupts Sinclair and begins to spill her guts. "Our friend Jana was hospitalized yesterday due to overdosing on pills. We were also informed that she has been taking other drugs prior to her suicide attempt."

"She recently started drinking a lot, as was very depressed lately. She would even behave very aggressively at times. If she doesn't get the help that she need fast, we fear that she is going to harm herself again and it may be too late the next time," Christy adds. The therapist asks them several questions about Jana's history and behavioral problems, trying to give them the answers to what they can do to help.

"Ladies, can you tell me how long your friend has been acting differently?" Before the girls answer the question, the therapist gets a notepad out and prepares to write down everything important she needs to know. Sinclair and Christy reflect back as far as they can to give the doctor all the information that she could possibly use in trying to help Jana.

After they finish giving detailed information about Jana's past, the therapist commends the girls on their dedication to helping their friend. She seems very interested to working with Jana as her therapist. "You don't know how important it is, but many people deny help until it's too late to get the help that they need," says Dr. Cain. "I see this happening all the time with young ladies that are using drugs and refuse to get help when needed," she adds. "They tend to think that they are in control of their situation, and that they can stop anytime they want. In your friend's case, she became so depressed and started thinking that nothing else mattered, so she tried to commit suicide."

"So what do we do know?" says Sinclair. "Tell your friend that the two of you have found the right kind of help for her and see if she will accept it. Regardless of the matter, if your friend doesn't admit that she has a problem, then there's no helping her at all. The first thing that a drug user has to do is admit that they have that problem, and the next step after that is to seek the help on their own from people they trust," Dr. Cain explains.

"Make sure that she knows that you are really concerned about helping her and let her know that seeking help is for her own good. If you like, I can visit her at the hospital to talk to her," she adds. "That would be great!" Sinclair exclaims, relieved that her friend would be in good hands. "At least that will take the pressure off of us for a bit," adds Christy.

After about an hour and a half talking to the therapist, Sinclair and Christy gather their belongings and leave, on their way to visit Jana at the hospital. Dr. Cain informs the ladies that she will pay Jana a visit later in the day. When the girls arrive at the hospital, they go into Jana's room and are very surprised to see Jerome in her room. Jerome greets Sinclair and Christy with a hello and moves to the side of Jana's bed. Despite puzzled expressions on their faces, they are very happy to see Jana looking well.

"Hey girl, how are you feeling?" Christy asks. "I am doing great; my body is a little weak but I will recover. I know what y'all are going to say, so let me explain," Jana tells them. "Yes, we would really like to know what you were thinking about when you took all those pills," says Sinclair with a frown on her face. "Why do you look so unhappy Sinclair?" asks Jana. "Because you scared the hell out of us for no reason at all," Sinclair reprimands her.

"Look, I don't want to argue, so I will tell you what I was thinking," says Jana. As Jana begins to explain what happened, she realizes how easily she could have killed herself. "I was very depressed and it felt as if my body was in so much pain. I just wanted that pain to go away. I started feeling really disgusting and wanted to wash that disgusting feeling. All this was happening so fast and I wasn't in my right frame of my mind."

"So, I just took all my clothes off, filled the tub, grabbed some Tylenol and got into the water. I started crying and my mind was telling me that my body was aching, so I started taking the pills so that pain I thought I was having would go away. The pain was not going away, so I continued to take more and more pills until I passed out. So, I guess, that's how I ended up here, at the hospital."

"I know I have taken y'all through a lot since we have been in Atlanta, but everything is going to be ok." Sinclair and Christy stare at each other, shaking their heads, really wishing that they could believe Jana. Still, their hearts are telling them that things are not going to get better until she gets help. "Look, we hear you and everything, Jana, but you say the same thing every time and nothing really changes," Sinclair objects. "If you don't get help fast, you are going to find yourself in a world of hurt," adds Christy.

"We love you and we don't want anything tragic to happen to you," Sinclair continues. "You have made many promises to us before, but your behavior tells us differently," she adds. "All we are trying to do is help you better yourself,"

Christy interjects. "If we didn't care about you, Jana, we wouldn't be here, talking to you about seeking the help that you need." Jana looks away from Sinclair and Christy, hiding tears flowing down her face. "What do y'all want me to do?"

"We have spoken to a therapist this morning to see if she is willing to help you," says Sinclair. "Therapist?!" yells Jana. "What, y'all think that I'm fucking crazy or something? I'm not seeing a damn therapist!" "It's for your own good. She just wants to talk to you and give you an evaluation, that's all," Sinclair tries to calm her down. "We don't think that you are crazy; we simply worry about you because we love you," she adds.

Jerome interrupts Sinclair and Christy, after listening quietly for a while. "Excuse me, but maybe she just needs a little time to get over what she has been through. What good is it going to do for her to hear someone that does not know anything about her tell her something that she is not ready to accept?" he asks. Sinclair and Christy stare at Jerome, surprised that he had the nerve to interfere. "What good is it for you to open your damn mouth, given that you don't know our friend either?" shouts Sinclair.

"We are trying to help our friend and you are suggesting that she doesn't need to talk to anyone. How about you leaving us alone?" Christy joins in. "He was only trying to help," says Jana. "Help who?" retorts Sinclair. "That's not what we call help," says Christy. After some conversation with Jerome, Jana politely asks him to leave, promising that she would talk to him later. "I can't believe that he even had the nerve to say anything," says Sinclair. "I want to be helped. I would talk to the therapist and see where this will go," Jana agrees, much to their relief. "She will be here later today to sit down and talk to you," Sinclair explains. "We are glad that you are accepting our help," says Christy.

CHAPTER 8

Later that day, Dr. Cain arrives to visit Jana at the hospital. Entering Jana's room, she finds her resting on her side, facing towards the window. Quietly approaching her bed, Dr. Cain removes her purse and places it on the bedside table. Before she can say anything, Jana feels the presence and quickly turns to see who it is.

"Hello, you must be the doctor that is supposed to come and talk to me." "Yes, I am Dr. Cain. I guess your friends, Sinclair and Christy, told you that I would be paying you a visit today." "Yes, they informed me that you would be coming today. For what reason, I don't know." "Well, I am here to talk to you about some of your behaviors that your friends are disturbed by. I advised them that I wanted understand your situation fully, which is why I came to see you personally."

"My friends are just worrying for no reason. I was going through a lot and made a huge mistake by taking too many pills, that's all." "I don't think people make those kinds of mistakes without any agenda behind it. Your friends were afraid that you were trying to harm yourself; so if you don't mind, I would like to have this opportunity to talk to you and see if, indeed, you may need or want help."

Dr. Cain sits down next to Jana's bed, grabs her notepad and a pen, along with her tape recorder, and begins to ask

Jana a series of questions about her personal life experiences and her family history. Slowly but surely, Jana begins to open up to Dr. Cain.

"How old are you?" she asks Jana. "I am twenty two." "Have you ever used drugs of any kind?" "No," replies Jana. After Jana answers 'no' to the questions about her using drugs, Dr. Cain pauses to make sure that Jana is telling the truth. "Jana, I am not here to judge you. I am here to help you get the treatment you need. I'm not saying that you are lying, but from what your friends have told me about you, I'm hoping that everything you are telling me is the truth," she says.

"Don't be afraid to open up and talk to me about whatever it is for me to know." "I have smoked marijuana when I was back in college and may have my fair share of alcohol, but nothing more serious than that," says Jana. "What about your family history?" "What about it?" "Is there any history of any of your family members using drugs or having a drinking problem?" "What do my family problems have to do with me and my issues?"

"Sometimes, the problems in children can be the effects of what their parents have been through. Tell me a little about your family?" prompts Dr. Cain gently. Jana pauses for a minute to gather her thoughts and begins to tell Dr. Cain about her family. "There's really not much to tell." "Tell me what you want me to know." "My mom raised me pretty much by herself because my dad was not around. To be honest, I never saw my dad. I had a stepdad, but he was an alcoholic and he would sometimes come home and fight with my mom."

"Still, to this day, I have not seen or heard from my biological dad. He didn't even come to my high school or college graduation." "Is that the reason why you have been so depressed and feel so alone at times?" "That and everything else that has happened to me," says Jana. "Could you be more specific?" After thinking about her past and what she had been through, Jana starts to get very emotional and tears begin to roll down her cheeks.

Dr. Cain grabs her hand and starts to comfort her by rubbing her hand, telling her that it is ok to let those tears out. "Sometimes I feel as if everyone has given up on me, so I try to hide my sorrow by drinking and surrounding myself with my friends. All the relationships that I have had have been a failure. I want love and affection so badly that I tend to fall for any man that I think is interested in me," says Jana. "Because my family has never been very close, sometimes I feel that I can't be alone. I should have kept my baby." "What baby?"

Jana stares at Dr. Cain, wondering if she knew about the rape and the subsequent abortion from her friends. "You didn't know about that? I thought that my friends told you everything about me." "They told me a few things, but I wanted to hear what I needed to know from you. As I said earlier, I am here to help you and that means getting the information I need from you, the patient," Dr. Cain explains.

Jana starts telling the doctor about all that happened a few months ago and how she ended up getting pregnant. She goes on to tell the doctor that because of the way the baby was conceived she felt that she needed to get an abortion. Jana seems to have a lot of regret about not keeping the baby. Dr. Cain is listening to the very emotional Jana telling her story from her past.

"So, you think that you wouldn't be alone so much if you decided to keep the baby?" "I think that I would have been better off because I would have had someone that I love that loved me back." "Having a baby is a blessing, but having a baby just for those reasons is not what you need. There are a lot of people out here that feel lonely and want the love and affection from someone, but in reality, if you don't love yourself first, then how are you going to love someone else?"

"You also can't hide behind alcohol and drugs, because once that high goes away, then you find yourself back feeling the same way," says Dr. Cain. The doctor continues to inform Jana about the importance of living a stress-free life and how to better herself as an individual, instead of depending on the love of someone else. "You have to have trust in yourself and believe that you can become a better Jana. No one controls your life but you. Drinking is not the answer, nor is using drugs the way to go. Believe in yourself and trust that, no matter what happened to you in the past, you can move on and build a better future," Dr. Cain adds.

Jana is listening very closely to everything that the doctor is saying and begins to feel some hope. Her confidence in her ability to change her life around starts to grow. "Remember that everything happens for a reason. Look at your past as an experience that was necessary for you to become stronger." The doctor takes out her business card and hands it to Jana. "What is this for?" "That is my card with my contact information on it. I want to keep in touch with you to monitor your progress. I want to meet with you at least twice a month so that you can give me some great feedback."

Jana stares at the business card and then looks at the doctor. "Why are you doing this for me?" "Because I know that you are a great person that came across a challenge in your life and I believe that you are strong enough to get through this. This is just a minor hurdle that you have to get over and, once you can achieve that, it will be nothing but a straight path for you."

"I want to thank you for taking the time to come and talk to me. Aside from my friends, not too many people have taken the time out to show their concerns about me. I promise, I will take it day by day and focus more on getting better." "Just remember to surround yourself with positive people that truly care about your wellbeing, such as your friends." She gives Jana a hug, grabs her things and leaves the room, knowing that Jana is feeling much better than she did before.

Jana has been in the hospital for a few days now and it is time for her release. She makes a phone call to Sinclair to come and pick her up. Thirty minutes later, Sinclair and Christy are at her room to help her to the car. Jana signs all the release forms that are required and, due to hospital policies, is taken out of the hospital in a wheelchair. Christy opens the passenger side door and helps Jana into the car. Sinclair gets in the driver side while Christy gets in the back.

"So, how are you feeling?" asks Sinclair. "I feel much better than I did a few days ago. I just want to thank you girls for really being concerned about me, and getting me help with the doctor." "So, she did come and see you?" asks Sinclair. "Yes, and she was very nice too. She's really good listener and knows how to help." "What you mean?" says Christy. "She just had a way about making me feel comfortable inside and opening up to her."

"Sounds like that's how Derrick is making you feel," Christy says with a laugh. "So are you and the doctor going to get it on now Jana?" Christy asks, still laughing at her own joke. Not really taking it seriously, Jana responds. "Hell no, girl, I may have been a little out of my mind, but I am strictly into men." "Ok, enough with the jokes y'all," shouts Sinclair. "So what did the doctor tell you that can maybe help you?" asks Sinclair. "She just told me to take life day by day and to focus more on myself than worrying about my past situation, that's all."

Sinclair seems to be a little more worried about Jana's situation than Christy and Jana are. "This is not a time to joke and play," yells Sinclair. "You need to get better Jana. I mean, just a few days ago, you wanted to kill yourself, and now y'all think it's a joke!" she adds. "Damn, Sinclair, calm down," Christy interjects. "Everything doesn't have to be so serious with you," she says. "Nothing happened. I am alive," says Jana. "I know what I need to do, Sinclair. Stop being so serious all the time," she adds.

"I guess, you are never going to learn, and even if you do somehow, you are going to learn the hard way." "I just got out of the hospital and I already know what I need to do. I will listen to you and the doctor that I spoke with. I was told to live my life and try to be happy and that's what I am going to do from this point on," says Jana. "Sinclair, we were just joking. It's not that serious," Christy adds. "I have nothing else to say, so y'all can do what y'all want to do," Sinclair finally gives up.

For a few minutes, there is nothing but silence in the car. Sinclair turns the radio on to provide some relief from the silence. She begins to hum a tune, mocking a song playing on the radio. Christy calls her name to try and get Sinclair's attention, but she ignores her. Christy continues to mock her, but still no answer. Finally, she taps Sinclair on her shoulder. Sinclair turns the music down and asks Christy what does she wants. "I have a question to ask you," she says.

"That day, when I came to your apartment and Derrick was there, I asked him if he could be my personal trainer." "How is he going to have time to train you when football season is in?" "I'm pretty sure that he would find time to give me a few lessons. I need to know if it is alright with you for him to be my personal trainer," she says. "Look, I couldn't care less if he trained you. What do I have to worry about? Do I have anything to worry about?" "You ask me that as if you have a problem with me being around Derrick alone."

"If I had a problem with it, then I would just say it. You are my friend, so why would I think something like that would be a problem? Look, the way I feel now, I don't care what you or anybody else does. Everybody in here seems to think that this is the way to be, so if that's how it's going to be, then from this day forward, the only person I am worried about is myself."

"It's not that serious," says Jana. "It seems to me that the person that really needs the help is you," she adds. Sinclair gets a little annoyed and turns the music back up. For about twenty minutes, they drive in silence. Almost back to their apartments, Jana comes up with an idea for the girls to go out to eat later that night. Christy agrees, but Sinclair claims to have other plans. Although the girls don't know it, she plans to go to the movies with Derrick later that night.

The girls arrive to their apartment complex, and you can almost cut the tension with a knife. Jana gets out of the car and thanks Sinclair for coming to pick her up from the hospital. Christy also gets out of the back seat and tells Sinclair that she is going to go up with Jana for a while and that she will talk to her later. Without any response, Sinclair drives away.

"I hope that she gets laid tonight because our home girl is acting really crazy right now," Jana jokes, as they enter her apartment. Sinclair arrives at her apartment in a rush to call Derrick. "What is this that I hear you wanting to be Christy's personal trainer?" she asks without any greeting. Derrick tells her to calm down a bit. "Look, she was making reference that she needed to get into better shape and I told her that she could work out with me," he explains. "Do you have a problem with me and her working out together?"

"'Cause if you do, then I want do it. If you like, you can work out with us as well." Sinclair gets really quiet for a moment and tells Derrick that she is sorry for going overboard with this stuff. "Look, I am really sorry. I just had an argument with my friends a few minutes ago, and I am taking my frustrations out on you." Derrick informs her that everything is going to be ok and that she should get some rest before he sees her later tonight. "After practice today, I will come over, so that we can spend the night together. Until then, please try to get some rest."

Sinclair agrees and hangs up the phone to take a nap. Jana and Christy are at Jana's apartment, trying to figure out what they want to do tonight. Christy advises Jana that she just got out of the hospital and it is best that she get some rest before she starts going back out again. "I have been resting for the past three days and I'm all rested up. I don't want to be stuck in the house any longer," Jana complains.

Without any confrontation, Christy accepts the fact that Jana is not good at compromises. "Look, we can go get something to eat, and after that, I am coming back home," Christy suggests. "So, you are going to bail on me tonight? It's Friday and I want to do something fun. I want to go somewhere and listen to some music," Jana objects. "I'm fine with listening to some music in the comfort of my apartment," says Christy.

"How about you just stay at your apartment all together and I will go out by myself," says Jana. "Why would you do that Jana?" "If you can't go all the way then you don't have go at all." "Since you put it that way Jana, then I will do just that and stay at my place tonight." "I swear it's like yours and Sinclair's periods stay on every damn day." "I think that's my hint to go. Have fun tonight," Christy says while leaving Jana's apartment. "I need to get some new friends," Jana says to herself. She then picks up the phone and calls the only other person she knows in Atlanta, Jerome.

After talking on the phone with Jerome for a few minutes, he agrees to come pick her up to take her out. Jana quickly gets dressed, excited at the prospect of the night out. In the meantime, Sinclair is waiting for Derrick's arrival. Christy calls Sinclair to let her know that Jana is going out without her. Still tense from their earlier argument, Sinclair seems not to care about what Jana is about to do.

"Why are you telling me this?" she yells at Christy. "I just thought that you should know." "Well, apparently I don't need to know anything. I am no longer responsible for what Jana is doing. I just hope nothing tragic happens to her and my prayers are with her," she adds. "What are your plans for tonight?" she asks Christy, changing the subject. "I am just going to stay home and watch some movies all by myself." "Well, if Derrick wasn't coming over tonight, I would've come by to watch them with you."

"Hey, don't worry about me; you and Derrick have fun tonight." While still on the phone with Christy, Sinclair hears a knock at the door. "Hold on Christy, someone is at my door." Sinclair goes to the door to see who it is. She looks through the peep hole and notices that it is Derrick. She opens the door and lets him in. Sinclair embraces him with a hug and a kiss before continuing her conversation with Christy. "Girl, that's Derrick. I have to go and entertain him," she says to Christy.

"Wait a minute," Christy interjects. "Let me talk to Derrick for a minute." Sinclair hesitates for a moment but eventually hands the phone to Derrick. Looking puzzled, Derrick takes the phone from Sinclair. "Hello," he answers. "Hey, stranger! This is Christy." "What's up?" "I wanted to know if you were still ok for training me?" she asks. Derrick looks at Sinclair as Christy asks him that question.

"I have to check with my girl." Already knowing what the question was, Sinclair nods her head to signal that it's ok for Derrick to train Christy. "I guess, I am your personal trainer," he responds to Christy. "When can we start?" she asks. "We can start next week." Christy agrees with the schedule and ends their conversation. Still unsure about them training together, Sinclair seems a little bothered by that hookup between Derrick a Christy.

"What's wrong now?" he asks. "I don't know why she just couldn't get somebody else to workout with." "She does not know anybody else here, that's why." "Can't you get one of your friends on the football team to train her?" "Look, it's really bothering me that you don't trust me," says Derrick. "If we are going to be together you have to trust me. I trust you, so why can't you trust me?" he asks seriously. "I had this happen to me before with my last boyfriend. A close friend of mine at the time wanted him to workout with her and she tried to come on to him. That's why it's hard for me to trust anybody," she says.

"Well I'm not your last boyfriend. I'm your boyfriend now, and you can trust me. Now, can we cut to the chase and go see a movie?" Sinclair begins to feel a little better because of Derrick's genuine statement. She then grabs her purse and they leave for the movies.

Jerome finally makes it to Jana's apartment. "What's up gorgeous?" he greets her. "Are you ready to go out and have some fun?" "I've been ready ever since I left the hospital this morning," she responds. "What is it that you want to do tonight?" he asks. "I was in the mood to hear some music and grab something to eat." Jerome stares at Jana up and down. "I dare you to go somewhere with me." "Go where?"

"Today is my homeboy's birthday and he wanted to go to a strip club tonight and celebrate. I told him that I was coming to hang out with you, but he insisted that I come. I was wondering if you would go there with me, so that I wouldn't have to stay long." Jana stares at Jerome for a minute and then tells him that she is down for whatever. "Let's have a couple of drinks before we leave my apartment."

Jana goes into the kitchen and grabs a bottle of Vodka and some cranberry juice. Before they knew it, they had drunk two glasses of Vodka and cranberry juice and were feeling nice. "We need to go," Jerome suggests.

Jana grabs her purse and they leave the apartment. On the way to the strip club, Jerome makes a stop at the liquor store to get some more alcohol. He runs into a friend of his inside and buys some weed. After purchasing the alcohol, he comes back out to find some guys talking to Jana through the passenger side window. Not mad at all, Jerome embraces it.

Jana is feeling a little lightheaded from the drinks she had at the apartment. Instead of Jerome telling the guys to back up from his window, he gives them a business card and tells them to call him, without explain why. He puts his trick into reverse and heads to the strip club. On the way, he pours Jana some more alcohol. They finally arrive to the strip club to meet with his friends.

"Damn Jerome, who is that fine lady you have with you?" one of his friends asks. "She's a good friend of mine, that's all you need to know." Jana attempts to get out of the truck, but slips a little bit, and her dress comes up past her waist, revealing the red thongs she has on. She quickly pulls her dress back down, but not before all eyes are on her. "Damn baby, show it to the world!" one guy yells.

"Shit, they need you on the stage in there. Hell, I would give you hundred dollars if you show it to me again," he adds. Jana seems to be intrigued by the guys showing her so much attention. She begins to entertain the boys outside the club. "All I have to do is show you my thong and I get a hundred dollars?" "Yes," the man responds.

She agrees and flips up her dress to the cheers of the guys that standing out there. The man hands her a hundred dollar bill. Jerome comments that she made a hundred dollars in less than a minute, seemingly happy for her. "If you took this seriously, you could make a thousand dollars a night easily. I could manage you and we could both make thousands a week. I mean, do you want to work for someone else for the rest of your life?" "I don't want work for anybody, but I don't think that I could be a stripper," she says.

"To be honest, you just stripped a few minutes ago and made a quick hundred." Not really intrigued by Jerome's tactics to get her to strip, she politely asks if they could go into the club now. Once inside the club, Jana sees money everywhere—girls walking naked, dancing on poles and on stage. Jana seems to get a lot of attention as she is walking to her seat in the club.

"You are the best looking girl in here," Jerome compliments her. "You can do it if you put your mind to it." "I don't want to put my mind to it, so let's forget it," Jana cuts him off. As the night goes on, Jana is at a level she has never been before. She is up dancing, smoking weed with Jerome and his friends, and even making some new friends with some of the strippers.

One stripper in particular challenges Jana to do what she does. Jana agrees to the challenge and copy everything the stripper does. The stripper starts taking shots, and Jana does the same. Next, the stripper removes a piece of her clothing, quickly followed by Jana. It gets to the point where Jana is just in her red thongs, dancing amongst Jerome's friends. She even gives other strippers lap dances. Jana is totally out of control.

One stripper really seems to like Jana and they begin to really get into to each other. Jana and the stripper start kissing passionately. It gets to the point when the stripper starts kissing on her chest. Jana begins to feel really comfortable. "Alright, break it up," says Jerome with a smile on his face. "Enough with that porn stuff; time to get out of here."

The stripper even offers Jana to come back home with her, but Jerome interferes. "She is going home with me," he says. "If anybody is going to get some tonight, it will be me." It's about 5 o'clock in the morning, and Jerome is waiting patiently as Jana gets her clothes on. "Hey don't forget your money," he says. "What money?" "That money on the floor is for you. See, I told you, it was that easy to make money in here," he says.

"Just imagine if you did this on a weekly basis; you could make a killing." "How much is it?" she asks. "Count it," he says. Jana scoops up all the money off the floor and begins to count it. "Damn, this is well over a thousand dollars. How did I get this much? What did I do? I can't remember." "You just shook what your momma gave you," Jerome says, laughing.

"I guess, I owe this all to you," says Jana. "Right now, no, but eventually yes," he replies. "What does that mean?" "Never mind; let's get out of here." Jana and Jerome leave the strip club and go back to her place. When they arrive back to Jana's apartment, Jerome asks if he could come up with her. "I don't mind," she says. "Plus, you don't want to be driving back at this time of night anyway."

They enter Jana's apartment. Jana is still surprised at all the money she made in one night. "If only I could do this without stripping." "There is nothing wrong with stripping," says Jerome. "All you have to do is picture yourself dancing in front of your boyfriend." "The problem is that I am not dancing in front of my boyfriend, I'm dancing in front of an entire room of horny men," she says. "Tonight, I was way too drunk to remember anything that I have done, so I wouldn't know how anyway."

"No matter how you did it, you did it," Jerome adds, as Jana goes back into her bedroom to change into her bedclothes. Jerome is on the sofa, almost about to pass out. Jana comes back into the living room. "Why do I get the feeling that you want me to strip?" she asks. "Is that what you do? You find girls to work for you? Is that how you make your living, managing girls that strip?" "Call it what you want, but it pays the bills and I don't have to work for anybody," says Jerome.

"Plus I didn't say that you should strip, I just gave you another option." "How many girls do you manage?" "If you really want to know, I manage twelve girls." "Damn!" she shouts. "But I will tell you this; none of my twelve girls are as bad as you are!" "Don't try and butter me up," Jana objects. "No I'm serious."

Jerome pulls out his phone and shows Jana photos of the twelve girls that he manages. "They are cute," she says. "Yeah, but you are better looking." "Well, I wish you luck with that, but I'm not interested in being a stripper." "You would be my lucky number thirteen," he says, laughing. "You are funny," Jana jokes, as she gets up from the sofa and heads into her bedroom.

Jerome asks, "May I come with you?" "I don't think that's a good idea. You are welcome to come get a pillow and a blanket, so that you can sleep on the sofa." Jerome jumps up and goes into the bedroom to get the bedding. While in the room he makes his way to Jana's bed and sits on the edge. "May I help you?" she says. "Yes you may." "How?" she says. He reaches over and strokes her hair. He then starts massaging her back and her legs. Very gently, he turns her on her back and leans over to kiss her. Jana allows him to make his move.

After kissing her, Jerome stands up and removes his clothes. Jana stares at Jerome's body. He then hops in the bed to remove Jana's clothes. "Wait, do you have a condom?" Jerome reaches into his pants and retrieves a condom. Jana watches him as he puts on the condom. He then climbs back on top of her, kissing her lips and caressing her body. Jana moans to every caress he is applying to her eager body.

With her eyes closed, she says to Jerome, "I want you inside of me." She then spreads her legs so that Jerome can enter her. As he gently penetrates her, Jana moans. "I haven't had this feeling in a long time." Jerome continues to stroke her gently before beginning to hit her spot. After about thirty minutes of different positions, Jana reaches her orgasm, followed by Jerome. Afterwards, Jerome rolls over, suddenly exhausted and ready to go to sleep.

"I want you to know that I had a great time tonight," says Jana. "I enjoyed hanging with you as well." "Although I have a job, I would consider working as a weekend stripper for you." Surprised that she agreed to work for him, Jerome gets up and leans over to Jana, happy with her response. "Are you serious?" "If I do this, you have to know that it will be only for the weekends that I am not busy doing other things." "Look, you can start out slow, but if it starts to pick up, you may need to work more days," Jerome offers. "We will see," says Jana.

It's Saturday afternoon and because Jana and Jerome got in so late, they slept in pretty late. Jana gets a knock at her door. She jumps out of the bed to see who is at her door. "Damn," she says. "It's Christy." She yells through the door, "Just a minute." She then rushes back into the room to put some clothes on. Jerome notices her rushing. "What's wrong?" "It's Christy, and I don't want her to be all up in my business."

"How about you do me a favor and put your clothes on?" Not liking the idea of being rushed, Jerome gets out of bed and gets dressed. Impatiently waiting outside, Christy knocks on Jana's door some more. "Alright, I'm coming!" yells Jana. After she and Jerome finally get themselves together, Jana opens the door. "Girl, y'all not fooling anybody," says Christy. "Hello Christy, How are you?" says Jerome

With a grin on her face, she speaks back. Jerome smiles at the sarcastic gesture. "Well, look, I have to go," he says. "I will talk to you later." He gives Jana a hug and leaves. "What's up with that?" asks Christy. "Are you and Jerome an item now?" "We are going to be business partners." "What kind of business do you have in mind?" "I will be working with Jerome on the weekends." "Doing what?" "I went to the strip club with him last night and I am going to work with him, stripping in the club on the weekends." "Are you crazy?" "Look y'all agree to stay out of my life and let me make my own decisions, so please stay out of this one," Jana retorts. "If you don't mind, I need to take a shower." Christy is shocked and leaves the apartment with a blank look on her face.

CHAPTER 9

"What a great movie we saw last night!" says Sinclair. "Yes, I thought that it was pretty good myself," Derrick agrees. "Nia Long is my girl too," he adds with a little smile on his face. "I thought that I was your girl." "You are, but Nia is my Hollywood chick," he says referring to the movie "Love Jones" they watched last night. "Well you are the big football player, I'm pretty sure you can get a hold of her if you wanted too."

"Let me stop before this gets out of hand. It's just a movie," Derrick adds. "You are my one and only woman I want in my life." "I'd better be. Wow, I can't believe it's almost 1 o'clock. We slept this late into the afternoon." "I'm glad I did, because I could use the rest. With all that practice I had to do the past week, I can sleep all day," he says. "By the way, our first pre season football game is Thursday," notes Sinclair.

"Will you be able to come?" "I wouldn't miss your game for anything in the world," she responds. "If it's ok with you, I can have two extra tickets and we can call Christy and Jana to join us if you want to bring them with you." "I forgot that you have to have your girlfriend Christy come see you," Sinclair says in a sarcastic tone. "I was just assuming that you didn't want to come to the game by yourself, that's all." "You know what they say when you assume right? You make a fool out of yourself," she says. "Whatever; if you want to bring them, I will leave you a ticket plus two extra tickets for your friends, just in case," he says. "I will think about it."

"Well, I have to get back to my place," Derrick changes the subject, not wishing to start an argument. "I could make you something to eat before you go," Sinclair offers. "Thank you, but I have to get to the practice facility after I leave home to go over some film with the defensive coordinator. But I will keep that in mind the next time I am here." "Keep what in mind?" "You cooking me something to eat," he says, laughing. "What, you don't think that I can cook?" she teases him.

"I hope that you can. My mom always told me to marry a woman that can cook." "Well, your mother doesn't have to worry about me, because I can cook." "I'm not talking about cooking no scramble eggs; I'm talking about some real soul food," he teases. "Greens, macaroni and cheese, fried chicken, neck bones, homemade cornbread and all the other southern dishes," he adds.

"You obviously don't know me as well as I thought you did. My grandma is an excellent cook and she taught me since I was eight years old how to throw down in a kitchen." "Well, when you are not too busy one day, I want you to cook me my favorite dinner." "And what is your favorite dinner?" "I just gave you a list of things that I like. I am sure that you put something together." "I have no problem with that, as long as you buy the ingredients."

"Why do I have to buy everything?" "Because you want to eat it," she says with a smile on her face. "Deal! "Next Sunday, after your game, I will prepare that meal for you," she says. Derrick agrees, grabs his belongings and goes home.

After Derrick leaves Sinclair's apartment, Christy calls and tells her that she is on her way to visit her. Ten minutes later, she arrives at Sinclair's place. "Good afternoon," she greets Sinclair playfully. "What's up girl?" "You are not going to believe who I just saw leaving Jana's apartment." "Please don't tell me it was Jerome." "Yes; but the thing is that he was not just visiting today, he spent the night with Jana."

"Are you serious?" "I am serious as a heart attack," says Christy. "Do you think something happened between them last night?" "Knowing Jana, I'm pretty sure that she slept with him," says Christy. "She doesn't even know him and she's already sleeping with him that fast," Sinclair notes, clearly worried. "Well, as she said when she left the hospital yesterday, she is grown woman and we shouldn't get in her business. I am just going to mind my business and let Jana do what Jana wants to do," she adds.

"I'm with you on that one, girl. As you said before, I hope that nothing tragic happens to her, but I am no longer going to put my two cents in anything she does." "Anyway girl, did you come over here just to tell me that she slept with Jerome last night?" "No girl, it gets better." "What are you talking about?" "Well, after Jerome left, when I got over there, she told me that they went to a strip club last night." "Why would she go to a strip club?" "That's what I am trying to figure out." Sinclair is shaking her head in disbelief.

"What happened at the strip club?" "She was telling me how she was drinking and dancing and guys were throwing money at her, telling her to strip. Before she knew it, she was down to her thong." "What?" yells Sinclair. "Are you serious, Christy?" "I am dead serious. At least this is what she is telling me." "What happened next?" "She then goes to tell me how this stripper was coming on to her and they started kissing and fondling each other."

"That is just nasty," Sinclair says in disgust. "Do you think Jana may have a little lesbian inside of her?" she asks Christy. "If she does, that's something new to me." "Ok, continue telling me the story." "So, after all that went down, she started bragging how she made over a thousand dollars last night." "A thousand dollars?!" shouts Sinclair. "Yes, and she showed me the money. She had a bunch of one dollar bills."

"That's typical in a strip club." "But here is the biggest surprise of them all," says Christy. "After everything went down last night and with all the money she claims to have made, Jana then tells me that she is going to work with Jerome as a part-time stripper." Sinclair stares at Christy with a shocked expression on her face, very surprised at the news. "I can't believe this shit!" she yells. "Enough of this shit. When I see her, we have to talk, because that shit is unacceptable," she adds, shaking her head.

Thursday arrives and it is the day of Derrick's first pre season football game. Sinclair invites both Christy and Jana to the game. They all ride with Sinclair to the game. "I haven't talked to you in a few days," says Jana. "I've just been a little busy, that's all," Sinclair notes casually. "I heard that you have been a little busy too," she adds. "I've just been enjoying life." "I bet you have." "Now, what's that's supposed to mean?" asks Jana. "Oh nothing; look, I am just trying to get to the game and see Derrick play."

The girls drive for about fifteen minutes before arriving to the stadium. They pick up the tickets and follow the huge crowd into the entrance to find their seats. After a few minutes of silence, Jana offers the girls something to eat and drink. Sinclair and Christy refuse the offer. "Ok, what is the matter now? I think we just need to get whatever we have on our chest, off."

"I can't believe what you did at the strip club," says Sinclair. "What can't you believe?" "Stripping for money, that shit isn't cool." Jana looks at Christy, very surprised that she went behind her back and told Sinclair about her business. "What kind of man would ask you to work for him stripping?" Sinclair asks. "What kind of woman are you to strip anyway?" "I am a woman that doesn't want to be like her friends and work for someone else for the rest of her life."

"I am so sick of this shit, so before this shit escalates into something big, it's best for me to find a ride back home." With that, Jana gets up and leaves the game. After Jana leaves Sinclair and Christy behind, they get tuned into watching Derrick play. The crowd erupts to the entrance of their beloved Atlanta Falcons. "Who are they playing?" asks Christy. "I think they are playing the Washington Redskins," says Sinclair.

"Oh my God, Mike," says Christy. "Wow I haven't heard that name in a long time. When was the last time you talked to him?" asks Sinclair. "It's been almost two months." "Damn girl, that's a long time. I thought y'all hit it off pretty good back in Baltimore." "He had too much going on that I couldn't handle." "Like what?" "Mike seems to be just out for one thing and I'm not that type of person."

"All guys are just out for one thing; you just have to know your worth and make them wait if you really like them. After the game, maybe I can get Derrick to ask Mike to come over so y'all can talk to each other," Sinclair suggests. "I guess that will be ok with me," says Christy. The game starts and the crowd erupts again, as the Falcons player almost breaks away to score a touchdown on the opening kickoff.

"What position does Derrick play?" asks Christy. "He plays defense—cornerback or something like that." "Girl, you mean to tell me that you don't know what position he plays! You need to pay more attention to your man," Christy reprimands her with a smile. "Don't worry about me and my man. Your only concern should be getting up with Mike."

The game finally comes to an end. Washington Redskins defeated the Atlanta Falcons 24-13 in the pre season opener. "Man, that was a good game, even though Derrick's team lost," says Sinclair. "Well, they did lose to the team we had cheered for while we were growing up," adds Christy. "Well, they are no longer my team," says Sinclair, referring to the Washington Redskins. "I guess we have to go down to the field and wait for Derrick to come out."

Sinclair and Christy grab their purses and go down to the lower level of the stand to try to catch up with Derrick. They wait for about twenty minutes before they start seeing the football players come out from their locker rooms. After about five more minutes, Christy finally spots Mike, standing on the field, talking to the reporters about the game they just played. After a few more minutes, out comes Derrick from the locker room.

Sinclair quickly calls him over. "I'm sorry about the game," she says to him. "No problem; it's not like it's a regular season game, but it clarified some things that we as a team have to work on," he says. "Hey Christy," he yells to her. "What's up, big man?" "If you like we can work out on Fridays, Saturdays, and Sundays." "That works for me." "Give me your number and I will call you and let you know when I am on my way," he suggests. Christy and Derrick exchange numbers while Sinclair observes very quietly. "Tell Mike to come over here," she interrupts, trying to change focus.

Derrick goes over to get Mike and brings him back over to Sinclair and Christy. "Well, well, well," he says out loud. "Look what's before my eyes. I never thought I would see you again!" For a few seconds, Christy doesn't respond. "Well, it's not my fault that you stopped calling me. The last thing I remember was you saying that training camp was approaching and that you were going to be very busy." "I didn't mean that I would be too busy to talk to you," he says with a smile.

"Anyway that's in the past; what's up with the present?" Mike asks playfully. "The present is that you can take me out to get something to eat." "Dang, I should have known that you would come at a brother like that! The first time you see me, you want me to take you out." "You just ask me what's up with the present and I'm telling you that at this present time you can take me to get something to eat," Retorts Christy.

After going back and forth, trying to come up with a plan, Derrick and Mike offer to take Sinclair and Christy out for food and drinks. "Since this is your city now, Derrick, where is a good place to go?" asks Mike. "We can go to the Cheese-cake Factory," he suggests. After deciding where to go, Mike rides with Derrick and Sinclair and Christy follows behind them in her car. They arrive at the Cheesecake Factory about twenty minutes later. "This is a nice place," Sinclair notes, looking around. "Is this where you take your groupies," she adds in a smart tone, looking at Derrick.

"How long are you going to keep giving me grief about me being a football player and these so called groupies?" "Calm down baby, I was just joking," she says. The waitress comes over to take their orders. Christy orders a pasta dish, but Derrick quickly disapproves of her choice. "Being that we are going to start working out tomorrow, I don't think you should be consuming so many carbs. Maybe you should have some baked chicken or salmon with a side salad," says Derrick.

After Derrick suggest what Christy needs to eat, Sinclair gets really jealous and stares him down. "What, are you her nutritionist now?" "Why are you getting so uptight Sinclair? If she is going to train the right way, then she needs to start eating right. That's all I am saying. Am I right Mike?" "Man, I have nothing to do with that. That's between you and your girl," he says.

"Sinclair, it's not that serious. He was just trying to give me some advice," Christy interjects, seeing that her friend is upset. For the remainder of the night, Sinclair decides to stay silent. Derrick tries to break her silence by trying to talk to her, but Sinclair is not saying a word. "Damn dog, I didn't think that going out to eat would be like this," Mike starts to complain. "Maybe we need to do this another time," he adds.

"You sure know how to spoil an evening, Sinclair," adds Christy. "It was not cool to get mad over something that simple. It's not that serious." Without saying a word, Sinclair gets up and walks out of the restaurant, with Derrick close behind her. "Sinclair, wait up!" he yells after her. "What is the matter with you?" "I just have a lot on my mind right now." "A lot of stuff like what?" he asks.

"Look, if you are still feeling uncomfortable about me training Christy, then I won't do it." "Do you think this is about Christy?" she asks. "I just have been thinking about everything since we have moved to Atlanta. Nothing seems to be going well. I miss being back home with my grandma and I miss my little sister as well. Christy, and Jana and I have been doing nothing but arguing since we came down here," she says, her voice trembling.

"This move was supposed to be a positive change, after all that happened in Baltimore, but everything seems to be going wrong. We were all so close back at home and now I feel like everything is going badly for us. Maybe this move wasn't the best choice for me after all." Sinclair starts crying, as the memories of the drama they experienced since moving to Atlanta start coming back. Derrick hugs her tightly, trying to calm her down.

"Look, everything is going to work out," he tries to reassure her. "You just have to believe that it will and stay positive." He kisses her on her forehead while rubbing his hands on her back. "Let's just try to relax and enjoy the rest of the night," he says. Sinclair looks up at Derrick, gives him a kiss. "Thank you for being here for me." They then walk back into the restaurant to rejoin Christy and Mike.

It's Friday afternoon, and, as promised, Derrick calls Christy for their workout. "Hey girl, are you ready for me to come and get you?" "I just have to put on my gym clothes and I will be ready," she responds. "So where are we working out?" she asks." "There's a gym located at my condo that has great exercise equipment. Just be ready and I will come by and pick you up."

Christy hangs up the phone and goes to get dressed for the workout. Soon, Derrick pulls up at the apartment complex and calls her cell phone to let her know that he is waiting for her downstairs. Christy runs out of her apartment to Derrick's car and gets in. "Damn girl, what do you have on?" he asks referring to Christy's long fitted tights and sports bra she has on.

"Just my workout clothes; what, you don't like what I have on?" "No, you are good," he responds admiring her body. "You're not going to stop by and see your girl Sinclair before we leave for our workout?" Christy asks him, as he starts to drive off. "That would not be a good idea," Derrick responds dismissively. "Why do you think that?" "I don't feel like hearing her saying negative things and giving me grief for working out with you. Plus, we have a lot of work to do today." "I hope that you will not be trying to work me crazy today." Christy teases.

"Are you afraid of a little hard work?" Derrick looks at her in surprise. "I'm not afraid, but I'm not stupid enough to work extremely hard for the first time." "Don't worry, I want let you go overboard. I promise that it will be worth it when we are done."

They arrive at Derrick's condo downtown. "I have to stop by my place to grab something. I will be really quick, I promise," he says. "You don't mind do you?" "Not at all, just go and handle your business," she replies. "You can come up if you like." Christy goes up with Derrick to his condo. She is very amused by what she finds. "Nice place." "This little old thing! It's nothing," he replies.

"I just got this condo because I was traded and never really had time to go purchase a home. So, for now, I am going to hold on to this until I buy my home." "I would love to have a place like this all to myself," says Christy. "Sinclair seems to think that it's too small for me. She calls it my bachelor's pad." "Well bachelor pad or not, I would love to have this condo," Christy repeats.

"Let me show you around my place," Derrick offers and gives Christy a tour around his condo, pointing out some important aspects of it that assumes she'd like. The more things he shows her, the more intriguing his life becomes to her. "Now that I have showed you my home, you may have a seat while I change into my workout clothes."

As Derrick goes into the bedroom to change his clothes, Christy picks up a photo album that has Derrick with his shirt off at the cover. "Damn, this man is fine!" she notes to herself. As she is looking at the photo album, she is not aware that Derrick is standing behind her. "Shit, you scared me," she yells. "I see that you found my photo album," he says. "Very nice," she responds.

"Me or the photo album?" he says. "Both," she replies. "You are not bad yourself," he retorts with a little smile on his face. "What are we doing? We need to go to the gym and get our workout in," she says. They leave Derrick's condo and go to the gym. "The first thing we are going to do is stretch," he tells her. "Get down on the floor, put your legs together and touch your toes." "I might not be able to touch my toes, but I will try," she says laughing.

After some stretching of his own, Derrick sits across from Christy to help her stretch more. He tells her to press her feet to his and grab his hands. They stretch a few more minutes then make their way to the treadmills. "We are going to run for about ten minutes and then we will do some abs work," he explains.

After ten minutes of running on the treadmill, Derrick guides her to the abs machine. "I am so winded," Christy starts to complain. "You are going to feel like that at the beginning, but you will get used to it." They are now at the abs machine and Derrick instructs her how to do crunches properly. "I tell you what, let's just do the regular crunches on the floor," he tells her after seeing her struggle with the equipment.

"Lay flat on the ground on your back, put your hands behind your head and raise both of your legs coming towards your elbows." At first Christy has a little problem with this but she later gets the hang of it. Derrick becomes a little touchy with his hands on Christy; but Christy seems not to mind.

After about an hour and a half of working out, Derrick and Christy are very exhausted and sweaty. "I am so sore," she says. "You didn't tell me that it would be this hard." "No pain, no gain," Derrick jokes. "I can use a cold shower right about now," she says. "If you like, you can take a shower at my place." "I don't think that would be a good idea." "It's just a shower," he says. "Plus I don't have any clothes to change into."

"I may have something upstairs that you can change into," he offers. After minutes of deciding whether to accept the offer, Christy makes up her mind and accepts. They get back to his condo and he shows her where he keeps the towels and soap. Christy goes into the bathroom to take a shower. Five minutes after Christy has been in the shower, in comes Derrick, already with his clothes off, and gets into the shower with her.

"What are you doing?" she asks. "I think we have chemistry here, and I want you so badly," he says to her. "This is not right; you are with my best friend." "I won't tell if you don't." Very shocked that Derrick has joined her in the shower, Christy still responds, when he comes close to her and begins kissing her lips and neck. Although she know that what they are doing is wrong, Christy doesn't deny the fact that Derrick's kissing and touching are fascinating. Before she knows it, she is seducing him too.

"I can't believe that this is happening," she says. Derrick tells her not to think about it and go with the flow. With his strong hands, he lifts her up onto his waist. The shower water is cascading down their bodies and steam from the shower is fogging up the glass. He penetrates her with aggression. Christy moans out loudly. The sex gets so intense that she has to put her fingernails into his back.

"Derrick stop!" she yells. Ignoring her wishes, he continues to penetrate with more aggression. "I know that you want it," he moans. "I'm going to give it to you too." Christy continues to try to stop him, but Derrick doesn't obey. "You don't have a condom on," she cries out. Still with no response, Derrick continues having sex with her. Christy begins to cry as Derrick refuses to stop.

After a while Derrick, comes to a halt. He removes himself from inside Christy and gets out of the shower. Christy then slides down the shower into a fetal position holding her hands to her face, tears streaming down her cheeks. Derrick grabs a towel and puts it around his waist. He then looks into the shower at Christy. "I guess you are going to tell your girl on me," he says. "Who do you think she is going to believe, you or me? I guess you'd better keep this between us. Now dry off and get dressed so I can take you home," he orders dispassionately. Christy gets out of the shower to dry off and puts on her clothes so that Derrick can take her home.

After a couple of days go by, Sinclair begins to notice a change in Christy. "You have been acting strangely lately," she says. "Why haven't you and Derrick been working out?" "I just been busy and really have not had time to work out." "Did something happen between y'all?" "Look, nothing happened, I just have been busy. Can we just not talk about this right now?" "Ok, no problem. We can change the subject," Sinclair responds.

"Have you spoken to Jana lately?" asks Sinclair. "No I haven't. I guess she's out with Jerome or maybe she's at home," Christy says dismissively. "I haven't spoken to her since she left us at the Falcon's game. I guess we can go check on her if you like," says Sinclair.

Sinclair and Christy go and visit Jana. Much to their surprise, when the girls knock on the door, they find that Jana is at home, but is not alone, as Jerome is there too. Before Jana let's them in, she gives them some rules to follow. "Please don't come in my place with your noses all turned up. Second, do not try and tell me that what I am doing is not best for me," she says.

After they agree follow those rules, she lets them into her place. When Sinclair and Christy come into her living room to have a seat, they are greeted by Jerome. "Hello ladies," he says. With a little hesitation, the girls respond. Jerome feels the awkwardness and begins to plead his case. "Look ladies, I am not a bad person." "Then what are you?" asks Sinclair, unable to hold it back. "I'm a business man," he responds. "You call what you do business?" Christy joins in accusingly.

"Everything I do is business. Y'all may not like it but for me it's business." "Well I don't think its business for some man to go around and pimp girls for money," says Sinclair. "What I do is none of your business. You need to mind your own business." "My fucking friend's business is my business and I don't like the fact that you are trying to get her to do your dirty work for you," shouts Sinclair.

"Jana, how could you even deal with a man like him?" Jana ignores Sinclair and the argument that her and Jerome are having. "Jana is not in this," says Jerome. "This is between me and you," he adds. "Every since I met y'all, you are the only one that have been giving me a hard time and that shit needs to stop," he yells at Sinclair.

After Jerome says that, Sinclair jumps up and gets into his face. "Who the fuck are you to tell me what not to do?" Christy jumps up to grab Sinclair, trying to calm her down. "Calm down," she yells. "I'm not calming down. I don't like the fact that he is corrupting my friend, acting as if he knows what's best for her," she says.

Jerome jumps up in Sinclair's face, tired of her running her mouth. "What the fuck are you going to do about it?" he asks with his finger pointing directly in her face. "Get your nasty ass hands out of my face," she yells. Jerome ignores her and continues to put his hands in her face. Sinclair pushes Jerome hand away from her face. Christy grabs Sinclair, desperate to stop the fight from escalating.

"Jana, are you going to let this man put his finger in my face like he's crazy?" Sinclair turns to Jana accusingly. Jana stares at her with silence. "Oh, you are just going to stand there and refuse to say anything to him!" Sinclair snorts. "Look, I told y'all before you came in here not to be starting any bullshit and you did it anyway," Jana replies. "We have been friends since we were kids and that's all you have to say to me!" Sinclair yells "This man has a point, y'all have been giving him a hard time every since we met him," Jana retorts.

With disbelief on her face, Sinclair shakes her head shocked by Jana's attitude. "As far as I see it, you owe him an apology," says Jana. "You are fucking crazy, Jana. I am not going to apologize to him for anything in the world; and if you choose this man over your friends, then I don't think that we should be friends anymore." "If you want to take it there, Sinclair, then it's your call," says Jana.

"Look, I think y'all should just chill out before this gets out of hand," Christy chips in. "We are too good of friends to let some man come in between our friendship," she adds. Jana sits down and stares at Sinclair and Christy, shaking her head, with a grin on her face. "What's so funny?" asks Christy. "As if you don't know," she responds. "Why don't you tell Sinclair why you haven't been working out with Derrick the last few days?" says Jana.

Christy is shocked to see what Jana has up her sleeve. "Tell her about the night you called me crying your little eyes out." "What is she talking about?" asks Sinclair. Christy is starring down Jana, shaking her head. "I mean, if this shit is about to blow up, then let this shit explode," Jana adds, sipping on her a glass of wine.

Sinclair stares back at Christy, trying to figure out what she is referring too. Christy begins to cry and is very hesitant to tell Sinclair what happened between her and Derrick. "There's no need to cry now," says Jana. "I'm sick of this whole shit. Do you want me to tell her what you told me?" asks Jana. "Alright!" yells Christy.

Christy looks into Sinclair's eyes, as her tears get heavier and heavier. "I'm sorry, but it wasn't my fault," she says. "What wasn't your fault?" asks Sinclair. "That day after Derrick and I worked out, he came onto me at his apartment." "What, are you fucking me? What do you mean he came on to you?" "He let me use his bathroom to take a shower and, while I was in there, he got in with me. I told him to get out, but he refused to, and he came on to me. I tried to make him stop, but he wouldn't stop."

"You expect for me to believe that shit, Christy! I knew all along that you wanted Derrick and you went behind my back and fucked my man," Sinclair starts yelling. "I will never forgive you for this shit, Christy; never!"

Sinclair grabs her cell phone to call Derrick. "I just want you to know that what you and Christy did was fucked up and you don't have to worry about messing with me again," she yells at him as soon as he answers his phone. With that, she hangs up on Derrick and turns her attention back to Christy. "I never in a million years would have thought that you would betray me like this Christy. Still, I learned from all of this that, no matter what, you can't trust anybody."

Christy interrupts Sinclair trying to plead her case. "It wasn't my fault. I tried to make him stop." "You just don't get it," Sinclair interrupts her angrily. "I don't care whether or not you tried to make him stop. The fact that you put yourself in that situation is inexcusable. You had no reason to go into his condo, let alone use his bathroom to take a shower. Regardless of whose fault it was, it still happened."

"After going back and forth over whose fault it was, Jana jumps up to end the drama between them. "Ok, enough with this Oprah shit! Y'all have to take this shit somewhere else!" she yells. Sinclair stares at Jana with a smile. "What bitch, are you going to judge me now?" Jana asks her, challenging Sinclair to an argument. "From the looks of it, I don't need to judge you. You made your decision." "Whatever you mean by that, you can take that shit with you," retorts Jana.

"It looks to me that our friendship has been tarnished and, on that note, I wish y'all all the best." Sinclair stares at Christy and Jana one last time and exits Jana's apartment. A few seconds later, Christy leaves as well.

CHAPTER 10

After a couple of days of crying and feeling betrayed, Sinclair desperately tries to put her life back together. As always, when she begins to feel down herself, Sinclair calls the only person that she can talk to about anything—Grandma. Sinclair gathers herself together and makes the call to her grandma.

"Hello Grandma," she says after Grandma picks up the phone. "How are you?" she responds, sensing something in Sinclair's voice. "I'm not doing all that well." "What's the matter?" "Every since I have came to Atlanta, things have not been working out for me." "What do you mean?" "I can't seem to trust anybody anymore." "Tell me what you are talking about."

Sinclair takes a breath for a moment before she begins to tell Grandma everything about her move to Atlanta. "For starters, Christy, Jana and I are not friends anymore. We fell out." "What happened?" "First of all, as soon as Jana got here, her entire attitude changed. She has been way out of control with everything. It has gotten to the point to where I can no longer be friends with someone that does crazy things and hangs out with people that are a bad influence on them."

"I'm a little confused," interjects Grandma. "Be more specific," she advises Sinclair. "Jana hooked up with this guy

Jerome, who convinced her to work as a stripper for him, and when I tried to tell her that it was wrong, she basically sided with him and chose him over our friendship. I can no longer be friends with someone like that, Grandma." "I can't believe what you are telling me! I mean, I can't believe that Jana would act in such a way. Not to mention that she would do something that would cause y'all to ruin your friendship."

Grandma can tell that Sinclair is very upset and disappointed in how things have been going since she and the girls moved to Atlanta. "Just try and calm down." "I'm trying, but every time I think about what has happened, I get so mad and sick to my stomach." "Just try not to let it get you down to the point where you are not focusing on your life. I'm pretty sure that there is something else that you would like to tell me," says Grandma.

Grandma can clearly hear Sinclair becoming very emotional on the other line. She continues to try and calm her down. "Calm down and finish telling me everything," says Grandma. "Just when I thought that it couldn't get any worse than what Jana has done, Christy did something much more disappointing."

"I have been seeing this guy Derrick for a couple of months and everything seemed to be perfect between us. Just when I began to feel that I could trust him, I got stabbed in the back by the one person that I would have never thought would betray me—Christy."

Grandma is very shocked at the news. "You and Christy and even Jana have been friends since y'all were little girls. I don't know why they would act in such a way and jeopardize y'all friendship." "I have to finish telling you what happened," Sinclair interrupts.

Before Sinclair can go into details about what happened with Derrick and Christy, Grandma interrupts her. "There's no need to go into details, I can read between the lines." "Why are these things happening to me Grandma?" "I know it hurts baby, but you have to remember that things are not always going to go your way; or, better yet, you are going to be disappointed at times in your life."

"What you have to understand is that, no matter how bad things get in life, you must not let it bring you down. Always remember that the only true person that you can trust is God and He is the only one you can give your all. Never put faith in a man because man will let you down always."

Grandma continues to give Sinclair a lecture on the importance of life. As always, Sinclair begins to feel a little better when Grandma is giving her advice. "Although Jana and Christy have done those things to you, you have to forgive them and pray that everything will work itself out. As far as Derrick is concerned, you have to also forgive him. Still, as a woman, you have to know your worth."

"If he is not the man that can treat you the way you want to be treated, nor is he going to respect you like you should be respected, then you let him go and you move on. Remember, at the end of the day, you have to make sure that you are well taken care of." For a few more minutes, Grandma continues to lecture Sinclair about life lessons before she breaks news to her about Uncle Pete.

"I have something that I need to tell you about your uncle." "What about Uncle Pete?" "You may have not known, but for a long time now, he has been a little sick," says Grandma. "What do you mean 'a little sick'?" Sinclair begins to get a little nervous, wondering what Grandma is about to tell her. "For months now, Uncle Pete has been battling prostate cancer. It's gotten to the point to where surgery is not going to help him."

"I never knew that Uncle Pete was sick. Why didn't you tell me this before?" "It was Pete's decision not to tell you and Tiffany. He didn't want y'all to worry about him, given that y'all have been through such a rough time in your life already." "Is he going to be alright?" "To be honest with you, Sinclair, it's not looking too good right now."

Sinclair bursts into tears, shocked to hear that Uncle Pete is so ill. "What are the doctors going to do now?" "They will start with chemotherapy immediately to try and see if they can get a hold of the cancer." "Maybe this would be a good time for me to come home," says Sinclair. "There is no reason for you to come home Sinclair. Don't use your uncle's situation as an excuse to run from your problems."

"I don't mind you coming to visit your family because you miss us, but to move away and not even try to make it work in Atlanta would not be the right decision to make. The devil is trying to work on you and you can't let him win. Promise me that you are going to give Atlanta another chance and make the best out of the situation that you are going through." Sinclair promises to Grandma that she will hang in there and not run from her problems.

Sinclair asks to speak to Uncle Pete, but Grandma informs her that he is not at home. "Could you have Uncle Pete call me when he gets back home?" Sinclair asks. "I most certainly will," Grandma agrees. "This is what I want you to do in the meantime—I want you to find a church home and get the word from the Lord. You must remember to seek God first and he will make a way for you."

"The second thing I want you to do is get involved with helping out in the community, like you did when you were here in Baltimore. One thing you have to remember is that you have to keep busy when things are not going your way." Sinclair takes in everything that Grandma is telling her. "You always loved to help out in shelters, so try and find a home-less shelter there and volunteer to help out on a daily basis." "What should I do about Christy and Jana?"

"Remember what I told you earlier in our conversation. You have to forgive them and leave the rest in God's hands. Give yourself some time to heal and decide if your friends are worth your friendship. Maybe after some days go by, then y'all probably can sit down and talk about some things. Right now, take some time for yourself and get to know you a little better."

Sinclair agrees to find a church home, help out in the community and takes some time to herself before hanging up the phone with Grandma. "Tell Tiffany that I love and miss her," she says to Grandma before getting off the phone.

A couple of months have passed, and the holiday season is approaching. It is November, and Sinclair has pretty much taken Grandma's advice. Since their conversation, she has found a church home to attend on a regular basis and has been volunteering at a local homeless shelter downtown. There have been several attempts by Christy and Jana to contact Sinclair too. There have even been times where they would pop up at her apartment, but there would be no response from Sinclair. Sinclair has totally removed herself from their friendship.

Derrick has also tried to contact her, but she refused to talk with him. It's now a week before Thanksgiving and Sinclair has been volunteering really late into the night at the homeless shelter, sometimes as late as 10 o'clock at night. The late hours started to take a toll on her, but because of her dedication and it being so close to Thanksgiving, Sinclair pushes herself to continue working without a respite.

Two days before Thanksgiving, Sinclair was working really late to prepare for the annual Thanksgiving feed the homeless feast. She is now pretty much the only person left to lock down the kitchen. After a few minutes of cleaning up and putting away things, it is time for her to lock up the place and go home. Sinclair grabs her purse and car keys and proceeds to the parking lot to get into her car. As she walks to her car, she is approached by a homeless man, asking her for money, to get something to eat. As she didn't have cash on her, she tries to explain to the man that she cannot help him, but he gets a little aggressive with her.

"What are you doing?" yells Sinclair. "I need money and I need money now," shouts the homeless man. "I told you that I didn't have cash on me, so please let me go." Sinclair then tries to pull away from the man, but he has a strong grip on her arm. He then pulls out a knife and shows it to Sinclair.

"I want money or I will cut you!" He yells coming closer to her. Sinclair gets really afraid and begins to shake nervously. She looks around to see if anybody can help her, but there was no one in sight. The man asks her again for some money. She denies him again. "Since you don't have any money, you are going to give me something else that I know you do have," he says. Sensing what his intentions are, Sinclair attempts to run, but trips in the process. The man picks her from the ground, and puts the knife to her neck.

"Please don't hurt me," she begs, crying. "Shut up and don't say a word!" he yells. He then tells Sinclair to dump the contents of her purse out onto the hood of the car to see what she has in it. Sinclair dumps all her belongings onto the hood of the car. Seeing that there is nothing of use to him, the man gets very upset.

"I should cut you for not having anything," he says. "What is it that you want?" "I need money for drugs and I need it now," he responds. "I'm sorry that I don't have any money for you to get drugs." Still with the knife pressed to her neck, the man attempts to take Sinclair behind an abandoned building.

She notices what he is trying to do and tries to escape once again.

As he attempts to take her in the back of the building, he threatens her some more. "You have something that I want." Sinclair begs and screams for help. He threatens her again with his knife and tells her that, if she yells or scream again, he would kill her. He finally gets her behind the building. With the knife still to her neck, he pushes her on the ground. He then jumps on top of her, lifting her dress up with his free hand.

With the same hand, he pulls down her panties. Very scared, knowing that there is nothing that she can do, Sinclair covers her eyes with her hand, letting the man to rape her. Afterwards, the homeless man runs away and Sinclair quickly gets up from the ground. She runs to her car and calls 911. About ten minutes later, police patrol cars and an ambulance appear on the scene. They find Sinclair is sitting in her car, crying and still shaking very nervously.

A police officer rushes to her car to check on her. "Ma'm, we are here for you, so please tell us everything that happened," he says. Still in shock and not able to say anything, Sinclair sits very still in her car, crying. "Ma'm, we need you to talk to us." Sinclair looks up at the officer. "I was raped," she yells and then grabs the police officer with into a tight hug. He then helps her out of the car and to the ambulance to be checked out.

A female EMS worker assists Sinclair. "Do you have anybody that you can call?" she asks kindly. Sinclair starts to think about calling Christy and Jana, but quickly erases those thoughts out of her head. "I have no one to call." "We have to get you to the emergency room," the EMS lady informs her.

After further investigations at the scene of the crime, they take Sinclair to the hospital and haul her car behind. Once at the hospital, Sinclair is put into a room and asked to put on a robe, so that the doctors can run further tests. They check her blood pressure, her temperature, her eyes and inside her mouth. They then check around the body for any cuts or bruises. The nurse then asks her to lay flat on her back and spread her legs apart.

She examines Sinclair's vagina, getting as many samples as possible. She notices semen inside her as well as some tears in the walls of her vagina. "We are going to run these samples to see if he had any STDs," says the nurse. With the mention of venereal diseases, Sinclair burst into a loud cry. The police officer that was at the scene of the crime enters Sinclair's room.

"I know that this is very hard for you, but we need to get some specific information from you regarding your attacker." Sinclair pulls herself together to give the officer as much information as she could. "I remember him having a big green jacket on, something similar to an army jacket. He had a black skullcap, and he was a tall black man. He had a thick beard, but I can't really remember much more."

"Is there anything else that you can remember, like a scar, a tattoo, or a cut he may have had on him?" the officer tries to jog her memory. She thinks for a minute and then remembers something else. "I do remember seeing a long scar that was on the side of his neck. That's all I can remember." The officer takes her statement down, telling her that they will look further into the case, and exits her room.

After spending the night at the hospital, Sinclair is released. Before she leaves, the nurse tells her that it will be a couple of days before the results of the tests would come back. She also gets a visit from the officers that were investigating the rape case. "With the description you gave us, we were not able to find a suspect yet. We will continue to investigate the case until we get a suspect in custody."

Sinclair thanks the officers and the nurse for their help and leaves the hospital. She arrives home twenty minutes later. When she gets into her apartment, she runs a bathtub full of water to take a bath. The thought of the homeless man raping her makes her feel really filthy. She hops into the tub, lays her head back, trying to relax, but can't help reflecting on what happened to her last night.

Again she begins to cry. "Why is this happening to me?" she cries out. "Have I done anything to deserve this treatment?" Those questions begin to run throughout her mind. As she is lying in the tub, her cell phone rings. She looks to see who is calling her. She recognizes Christy's ID, but decides not to answer her call. The thought of what Christy has done to her upsets her even more. The phone rings again and, this time, it's a call from Jana.

She refuses to pick up the phone once again. "Maybe I just need to go home for the holidays and get away from this city for a few days," she says to herself. She picks up the phone and calls her Grandma. "Hello Grandma." Grandma tells her that she was just about to call her. "What's wrong Grandma?" "Uncle Pete died early this morning," Grandma tells her through painful sobs. Sinclair burst into tears and tells Grandma that she is coming home as soon as possible.

The next day, Sinclair arrives home to Baltimore. She jumps quickly out of her car and runs into the house. She first gives her grandma a hug and then goes to kiss Tiffany. Seeing them again makes her very emotional. Grandma looks at Sinclair questioningly. "Everything is going to be ok." "So far everything has not been ok," Sinclair retorts. "I should have never left home in the first place."

Grandma grabs Sinclair and hugs her tightly. "It's not your fault that Uncle Pete is no longer with us. You have to remember that everything happens for a reason and you shouldn't blame yourself." She continues to shed tears while Grandma hugs her close to her chest. "When can I go see Uncle Pete?" "They have his body down at the mortuary, preparing it for the funeral on Saturday."

Sinclair sits down in a chair in the kitchen. Grandma then asks her if she wants her to fix her something to eat. "Right now Grandma, I don't have any kind of appetite." "You have to eat something. This can't be all about Uncle Pete. Tell grandma what is really bothering you."

Sinclair lowers her head just, as Grandma finishes asking her that question. "For a long time, I mean, all your life, I knew when something was bothering my baby." Grandma sits in a chair besides Sinclair at the kitchen table. "Now, tell me what's really going on." Sinclair pauses for a second and looks up at Grandma. "There's nothing to tell. I just have to deal with my issues on my own."

"It's better if you talk to someone. It might help you with whatever is on your mind." "What I really want to do now is go upstairs to my room and take a nap." "I think that will be a good thing to do and, while you are taking a nap, I will make you and Tiffany something to eat." Sinclair hugs Grandma and Tiffany again and goes upstairs to her room. Grandma stares at Tiffany.

"That girl has been through so much in such a short period of time. Promise me, Tiffany, that, if you ever have something you need to talk about, you will come and talk to me." Tiffany smiles at Grandma. "I will talk to you about everything." "Now, that's my baby." Grandma laughs and lifts Tiffany into her arms. "Well let's hope this dinner I am about to prepare cheers her up."

"Tiffany, would you mind helping your grandma prepare this 'welcome home' dinner for your sister?" asks Grandma. "I don't mind at all," Tiffany replies enthusiastically. Grandma and Tiffany gather the pots and pans and all the food from the refrigerator and pantry and start preparing the meal. As they are cooking, Tiffany starts asking Grandma a series of questions. "Is Sinclair going to be ok?" "Yes, she is going to be fine. Why do you ask?"

"Well when I gave her a hug, I saw a mark around her neck." "What kind of mark?" "It looked like a bruise." "I didn't see that. I guess I will check it out when she comes back downstairs." Grandma begins to worry about Sinclair. "I just hope that my baby wasn't involved in any kind of domestic violence."

A few hours later, Sinclair comes back downstairs from the long nap. She welcomes the aroma in the air, knowing that it promises an excellent meal. "You look well rested," says Grandma. "I needed that. It seems like I haven't slept in a long time. So, it smells as if we are having my favorite foods!" "You know that I have to cook your favorite foods when you come home," says Grandma with a smile.

"We have your greens, macaroni and cheese, fried chicken, homemade cornbread, and for desert, homemade apple pie." Sinclair rubs her hands together. "Let's get it on." "Well, I guess, I will say grace, since Pete is no longer with us." Before Grandma says grace, Sinclair jumps up and grabs an extra plate, fork, and glass and puts it in the place where Uncle Pete used to always sit.

"He will always be with us," she says with a slight smile on her face. Grandma proceeds on with the grace. After a few minutes into having dinner, Grandma begins to think about what Tiffany had told her earlier. Sinclair notices that Grandma is looking at her. "What's wrong Grandma?" "I didn't notice it before, but I see that you have a bruise on your neck. Do you mind telling me how that got there?"

"I just had a little accident last night, that's all," Sinclair tries to sound casual. "What kind of accident did you have that would put a bruise on the side of your neck?" Sinclair does not want to tell her Grandma the truth about what really happened to her, so she gives Grandma a lie. "I burned myself with the curling iron trying to get here as quick as I could." Grandma looks at her, certain that what Sinclair is telling her is not what really happened.

"Sinclair, I know when you are not telling me the truth. So, please now tell me what really happened to you!" "Grandma, I told you that I burned myself, that's all. Nothing happened to me besides that." "If that boy hurt you, you must tell me so," Grandma says, pointing her finger at Sinclair. Grandma is now certain that Derrick has abused her.

"Look, whenever you are ready to tell me the truth about what really happened to your neck, I will be ready for you; until then, we will stick to the story that you are giving me. I don't like it, I don't like it at all," she says with a deep angry tone. Thirty minutes later, they finish up their meal and clean up the kitchen. Sinclair begins to feel really badly about not telling her grandma the truth.

In all her twenty-one years of living, she always knew that she could tell her Grandma anything. But the matter is that so much has happened lately and telling her grandma that she had been raped would have devastated her. After accepting the fact that she has to keep this from her grandma, Sinclair goes back upstairs to unpack her suitcase. In comes Tiffany into her room.

"What happened to your hair?" she asks, pulling on Sinclair's hair. "What you mean?" "It looks that it could use another curling iron," she says laughing. "Were you not able to find a salon to go to in Atlanta?" "Unfortunately no; I guess we can go see Shannon tomorrow at Shay's Salon." Sinclair stares at Tiffany and then gives her a high five. "You know what? I think we both can use a hair do tomorrow, so you and I will pay Shannon a visit to get our hair done.

The next day comes and Sinclair and Tiffany go to Shay's Salon to visit Shannon. "Oh my God, look what just came through the door!" Shannon exclaims with a huge smile on her face. "I can't believe my eyes. What brings you back to Baltimore?" "Well, if you haven't heard, my Uncle Pete passed away." "I'm so sorry to hear that. How did he die?" "Uncle Pete had cancer that I didn't know about." "Are you ok?" "I will be fine."

Shannon gives her and Tiffany a hug. "I see something else has passed away too," Shannon says with a laugh. "What's that?" says Sinclair. "Your hair! How about you jump your tail into mu chair so I can bring it back to life." Sinclair gets into Shannon's chair to get her hair done. "I guess when you were in Atlanta you said 'the hell with it.'" "So much was going on down there that I didn't really have time to find a salon, so I would just keep it in a ponytail."

"I see that you have a lot of split ends that need attention. I guess, I have to go into my bag of treats and pull something out of there to help this hair of yours," Shannon jokes, as she in combing through Sinclair's hair. "Do whatever you need to do because I know my hair needs it." Shannon lifts Sinclair's hair up to put the apron around her neck. When she begins to tie the apron around her neck, she too notices the bruise.

"What happened to your neck?" "I burned myself with a curling iron." "Sinclair, I have been doing hair pretty much all my life and that's not a burn mark. That looks more like a knife cut," she says, pointing at Sinclair's neck. "So I am going to ask you again, what happened to your neck?" Sinclair gets very quiet and glances over at Tiffany, noticing that she is listening in on their conversation.

Sinclair jumps out of the chair and pulls Shannon to the side. "Ok, that's not what really happened to me, but I don't want Tiffany to listen in on this conversation." "Ok, then what happened to your neck?" "When the time is right, I promise I will tell you. Can we please not talk about my neck anymore?" Shannon agrees not to have anymore conversation about her neck and they both go back to Shannon's work station.

While Sinclair is getting her hair done, one of Shannon's customers shouts out to her. "Did you tell her about Precious?" Sinclair looks up with a frown on her face. "What about Precious? What's her story now?" Shannon shakes her head. "I knew that the lifestyle that girl was living was going to catch up with her some day." "What are y'all talking about?" Sinclair asks, still with a puzzled look on her face.

"Girl, Precious was coming in here, flashing money, new bags, shoes, clothes—you name it, she had it. I was wondering how she was getting all this stuff, but I never asked her. One day, she came in here to get her hair done; she pulled up next to the shop in a new black BMW. As I am doing her hair, about an hour later, the cops burst through the door. They started asking her questions but her answers didn't seem right to them. Girl they snatched her out of my chair and put handcuffs on her. Later, I found out that she was trafficking drugs for some new boy from D.C. that she had met."

Sinclair's mouth almost drops to the floor when she hears the news about Precious. "Well, I can only hope that, whenever she gets out, she would have learned from her mistakes," says Sinclair. "Well she has a long time to think about it, because I heard they gave her fifteen years fed time," Shannon says shaking her head. "Oh my goodness, that's a long time."

After the talk about Precious and the many other conversations that took placed in the salon, Shannon has finished doing Sinclair's and Tiffany's hair. "How much do I owe you?" "It's on the house. Just send my best wishes and support to your grandma for me and we will call it even," she says to Sinclair as she gives both girls a hug.

After leaving the salon, Sinclair and Tiffany go back home. "I don't want you to tell Grandma about anything you heard us talking about in that salon." "I thought that you burned your neck." "Look, I said that because I didn't want you are Grandma to worry about me." "Are you going to tell Grandma what really happened to your neck?" "I will in due time, but for now, I need you to promise me that you are not going to say anything."

Tiffany sits quietly before answering Sinclair's questions. "Tiffany, are you listening to me? I don't want you to say anything about the mark on my neck around Grandma. Do you promise?" "I promise, but I don't like the fact that you lied to Grandma." "Sometimes, to prevent hurting someone you love, you may have to lie. Depending on the situation, it can be good to withhold the truth." "Well I'm never going to lie to Grandma." "Well, let's hope that you are never put in that situation. However, if you ever experience what I have been through, you might reconsider that decision." Sinclair is silent for a moment. "You're right, lying is not a good thing to do, so don't do it. I will tell Grandma the truth when the time is right."

It's a day away from Uncle Pete's funeral and Grandma, Sinclair and Tiffany go to the mortuary to view the body. Tiffany seems to be a little frightened by seeing Uncle Pete lying in the casket. Grandma assures her that everything is going to be alright and that Uncle Pete is sound asleep.

"He looks so peaceful," says Grandma. "He had suffered so long and now he doesn't have to suffer anymore. His soul is in a better place now and God is watching over His son that He called home." Grandma rubs her hand onto Pete's forehead, looking at his body from head to feet. "The last time I was here was when I came with Mrs. Kathryn to view Kenneth's body," Sinclair says, as tears start running down her cheeks.

"I never thought that, only months later, I would be here, looking at my favorite uncle." Grandma puts her other arm around Sinclair and embraces her close to her side. "I want you to take Tiffany back with you to Atlanta." "Why Grandma?" she asks. "I'm getting a little too old to take care of her." "But you will be all by yourself then, Grandma. I can't let you be by yourself." "Listen to me, Tiffany needs someone strong to look after her, and although I am strong mentally, physically I'm not able to do it anymore." "Why don't you come with us then Grandma?"

Grandma laughs at the thought of moving away from Baltimore to Atlanta. "This is my home. I have never left this place; this where I was born and this is where I'm going to rest in peace." "How does Tiffany feel about moving to Atlanta to stay with me?" "Child, that little girl will be delighted to have the opportunity to stay with her big sister," Grandma reassures her with a smile.

"I just want you to be alright Grandma." "Don't worry about me, just make sure that you raise that little sister of yours to be a great girl." "I love you Grandma," says Sinclair while giving her a hug. When they get back home, Sinclair calls Tiffany to the living room. "Have a seat, my little sis." Tiffany is very confused when she sees Grandma coming into the living room as well.

"Did I do something wrong?" "No, no, not at all," says Sinclair. "What's this about then?" "Well, we were wondering how you would feel about moving to Atlanta with me." "Are you serious?" "Yes, I am serious." "I would love to move to Atlanta with you, Sinclair," she says, jumping with joy. "When do we leave, when do we leave?" she asks repeatedly. "Well, first, we have to take care of a few minor changes with your school and get all your records and transfer them to a school in Atlanta."

"Grandma also has to sign over legal guardianship to me and, I say, after the holidays, we should be ready to go." "I'm going to miss you, Grandma," Tiffany says while giving her a hug. After all the excitement, Tiffany runs upstairs to her room, singing a happy tune. "I told you that child would be ecstatic about going with you to Atlanta. She loves to be around her big sister." "I'm just surprised to see you let her go." "Well, you can't hold on to anything or anyone for too long. Plus, I think that you need here there with you because of all the stuff you have been going through. I think she will serve you justice." "I promise I will do a great job with her, Grandma." "I know that you will, baby. That's why I'm letting her go with you."

The day of Uncle Pete's funeral has arrived. The family prepare themselves for the service. After several hours of service, Uncle Pete is put six feet into the ground. Many tears are shed between Sinclair, Grandma and Tiffany, as they try to come to terms with the fact that Uncle Pete is gone. Eventually, they leave the cemetery and goes home. "What a sad day," says Sinclair.

It's been a month since Uncle Pete's funeral. It's a few days before the New Year and Sinclair has been running many errands to get the information that Tiffany is going to need to move to Atlanta. She collects her school records and medical records needed in order for her to get into a new school. When she arrives back home, Sinclair is not feeling so well. She runs quickly to the bathroom and starts throwing up.

Grandma hears her vomiting. She knocks on the door and asks Sinclair is she alright. "I'm ok Grandma." "You don't sound ok. Do you need me to get you anything?" "No, it's probably something I ate." She flushes the toilet and splashes some water onto her face. Moments later, she comes out of the bathroom. "Are you sure that you are going to be alright?" "I will be ok," she tries to reassure her grandma again, even though she suspects what might be wrong with her.

Later that day, Sinclair goes to drug store, thinking about the attack that happened to her. She buys a home pregnancy test and goes back home to take it. She goes into the bathroom and urinates on the stick. A few minutes later, the pregnancy test results come back and they are positive. Sinclair is pregnant. She begins to cry.

Grandma hears her crying and comes into the bathroom. She sees the pregnancy test on the counter. "What am I going to do now, Grandma?" "This is a decision you have to make on your own, but I will support whatever decision you make," she says, holding Sinclair in her arms. "I'm going to keep the baby," Sinclair replies, crying in her grandma's arms. Grandma decides not to question Sinclair about who the father is, but her gut feeling tells her that there is something not right about her surprise pregnancy.

CHAPTER 11

THE YEAR 2000

Almost three years later, Sinclair has a new life and two people that really depend on her—her two-year-old daughter Angel, and her sister Tiffany, who is now ten years old. This has been by far the biggest challenge in her life. She has vowed to do the best that she can to ensure that her child and her baby sister have good life. After all, this was a promise she made to her grandma. Over the years, Sinclair has become very antisocial, never really having time to enjoy life and do anything for herself. This has not been the life she has chosen, but she has accepted it nonetheless. For two years, she never reached back out to her friends for either comfort or support, but she did think about Christy and Jana quite often. Moreover, the fact that she doesn't have any idea who her daughter's father is upsets her greatly. As she reflects on all that has happened to her during the last two years, Tiffany comes into her room.

"I'm ready to go to school now." "Oh yes, it is the first day of school for you. Are you nervous?" "It's only the sixth grade. I will be fine." Sinclair laughs after Tiffany says that. "Well, let me get Angel ready and I will take you to school." Sinclair picks up Angel out of her bed and gets her dressed.

"How is my little Angel doing?" she asks, lifting her into the air. Angel is really enjoying the playful humor that Sinclair lavishes on her. After she gets her dressed, she prepares her breakfast and fixes Tiffany's school lunch. "You look very tired," Tiffany observes. "I'm just a little exhausted," she replies. "But I will be fine. You just enjoy your first day at school."

She loads the car with Angel and Tiffany, ready to drive them to daycare and school. "I have so much to do today," she tells Tiffany. "What do you have to do?" "I have to plan a party for this Saturday and I haven't even started putting everything together yet." Within the last year, Sinclair had started her own business, planning weddings and parties for people.

"I'm pretty sure that you will get it done on time," Tiffany says with a smile. "You're right. Still, I have to focus on my job more." After she drops the kids off, she begins her daily errands to collect the supplies she needs to set up the party. She arrives at the mall. After shopping throughout the store, Sinclair's feet begin to hurt badly. She goes to the food court to get a break from all the walking she has done. Less than five minutes later, she hears someone calling her name from behind her and turns to see who it is.

"Oh my goodness!" she yells, noticing Derrick standing behind her. He greets her and sits across from her at the table. "What are you doing here?" he asks. Silent for a moment due to the surprise, Sinclair finally responds, "I'm here gathering supplies that I need for this couple's party on

Saturday." "I can't believe that it's been two years since the last time I saw you," he says.

"Yes it has been a long time, but we both know the reason for that." "I never really had the opportunity to say how sorry I am for betraying you like that. It wasn't right and I should have known better." "I guess you got what you wanted." "I know things will never be the same between us, but I want to tell you that it wasn't Christy's fault. I am the one you should blame," Derrick tries to explain.

"What do you mean 'your fault'? It takes two to have sex," Sinclair retorts with a frown on her face. Derrick then tells Sinclair about everything that happened that day after he and Christy finished working out at the gym. "So you see, I came on to her. You and Christy have been friends for a very long time and I shouldn't have interfered. But, again, it was all my fault."

"I can't believe that you would stoop that low and hurt me like that. You had me going off on my friend for nothing, all because I thought that she was the one coming on to you!" "You have every right to be mad at me, but not Christy." Sinclair leans back into her seat with a disgusted look on her face. "What's wrong? What are you thinking about?" Derrick asks.

"All the time that I have missed with my friends and the new things that I have in my life now—that is what I am thinking about!" "What new things?" Derrick asks, a confused look on his face. "Well, my life changed dramatically." "How has your life changed? What are you talking about?" "Well, if you must know, I have a two-year-old daughter Angel and my little sister Tiffany has moved down to live with me."

"A daughter, wow! So are you married or with the baby's father?" "That is none of your business now." "You're right; it's none of my business. Still, congratulations are in order!" "Thank you," Sinclair replies. "How is the football thing coming along?" "Bad news; I'm not playing anymore." "What happened?" "A lot," he says shaking his head.

"A lot like what?" "Remember that knee injury I sustained back when I got into that fight with Kenneth? Well, let's just say that it came back to haunt me on the field." "I'm so sorry to hear that. Maybe it was karma; a sort of punishment for you doing what you did to me. As bad as it sounds, that may have been my revenge."

Derrick stares at Sinclair, very shocked that she would say such a thing. "I don't think that's the reason, but if believing it makes you sleep at night, you can have that." Sinclair smiles and he continues. "Well, anyway, during one game, some dude came out of nowhere and hit me below my knee, tearing it to pieces. The next thing I remember was being carted off the field with tears coming down my face. The doctors told me that I would never be able to play football again."

"So, without football, what are you going to do?" "Well I'm still in football, but I'm on the coaching staff with the team." "That's good news, I suppose." "It's not the same. I hate to watch and not be able help the team on the field." "You are helping by helping someone else get better. That's how you have to look at things. Everything happens for a reason and now you can use this opportunity to become a better coach than you were as a player," she says.

"That's one thing I miss about you. You always knew the right things to say." "Well like they say, you don't realize what you miss until it's gone." "I cannot agree with you more and I really do miss you." Sinclair and Derrick smile at each other, both thinking about the good times they once shared. "Hey, I have a question to ask you," he suddenly says, interrupting their reflective moment.

"And what is your question?" "I was wondering if, maybe, perhaps we can be friends again." "As long as you keep in your mind that we are only friends and that's all, then that's fine with me." "I can handle that. Being friends is better than nothing at all," says Derrick. "Well I must be going now. I have a million things that I need to get done." "Do you need any help with anything?" "See, you are moving too fast already! We just started talking again. But, no thanks, I'm fine."

Sinclair grabs her bags from the ground. "Oh, there is one thing that you can do for me," she says with a smile on her face. "What's that?" "If you talk to Christy again, tell her that I said hello." "I have a better idea. How about you call her and talk to her yourself. I'm pretty sure that she would be glad to hear from you again." "Does she have the same number?" "As a matter of fact, she doesn't, but I can give it to you if you'd like." "That will be fine."

Sinclair grabs her cell phone and adds Christy's new number into the memory. "By the way, I'm pretty sure that she has some news to tell you as well." "What kind of news?" "As I said, she will tell you herself whenever you decide to call her." Sinclair gets very curious to know what kind of news Christy may want to share with her. "Well, it was nice to talk to you and I hope that I will see you again. Now, I have to go and finish my errands. Not to mention that I have to pick up my two little girls from school later today." "It was a pleasure talking to you too, and I hope to talk to you again." Sinclair says her final goodbye to Derrick and exits the mall.

Later that day, Sinclair is back at home, preparing dinner for Angel and Tiffany. "So, tell me Tiffany, what happened at school today?" "Not too much; all we did was go over the weekly plan." "That's all, nothing exciting?" "Well, there was something a little exciting that happened today." "Tell me, I want to know." Sinclair takes a seat at the dinner table to hear what Tiffany has to tell her.

"Well, it was this homeless man that was hanging around the school and some of my friends and I started talking to him." "What is a homeless man doing around your school?" The thought of a homeless man makes Sinclair very weary, given her bad experience two years ago. As a result of trauma her rape has caused her, until this day, Sinclair has never volunteered nor helped any homeless person that she has come across.

"I don't want you messing around with no homeless person again," she starts shouting at Tiffany. "What do you have against homeless people?" "That's not up for a discussion. All you need to know is that I don't want you around them. They are bad and they are trouble, so stay away from them!" Sinclair jumps out of her seat and pushes it hard into the table. She pushes the chair so hard that Tiffany jumps back out of her seat and the baby starts crying.

"What did you do that for?" Tiffany asks in shock, as Sinclair grabs a sippy cup to give to the baby to stop her from crying. "I'm sorry Tiffany, but it's not safe to hang around homeless people." "Not all of them are bad. They just need a little help to get back on their feet," Tiffany says, pushing the chair under the table before running off to her room, clearly hurt and confused.

Noticing Tiffany's anger, Sinclair grabs Angel and follows her to the room. She finds Tiffany lying across the bed with her head in the pillow. "I'm sorry to have upset you Tiffany. But it's for your own good." "It's not for my good; it's really all about you. What has any homeless person ever done to you?" Tiffany asks, her voice full of anger.

Inside, Sinclair really wants to tell Tiffany what happened to her two years ago, but feels that it's not the right time to share that information. "Look, I've heard some really bad stories from people telling me what homeless people have done to them and I just don't want anything happening to you, that's all." "Nothing is going to happen to me. He just comes by our school, trying to find something to eat." "Well, they have shelters for that and if he needs something to eat that badly, then he can go there." "Are you telling me that it's not good to share and help people?"

"No I'm not saying that, Tiffany." "Then why are you telling me not to help this homeless man?" "Because he just may turn out to be a bad person; a lot of these homeless people are on drugs. They can lose their mind when they are using those drugs." "Well, you don't know if that is the case until you get to know them." "Listen to me Tiffany, and you listen good, I don't want you to involve yourself with this man. If he comes back to your school, asking for something to eat or money, then you go and tell the principal. I'm not going to sit up here and have this conversation with you all day about you helping a homeless man." Sinclair walks out of Tiffany's room, slamming the door behind her.

The next morning, Tiffany gets up a little early, before Sinclair awakens. She quickly fixes a lunch for her and packs some food for the homeless man, anticipating that he'd show up at her school. She bags them separately and puts one lunch into her book bag for the homeless man and keeps one in her hand so that Sinclair can see it. Just as she is done, Sinclair comes into the kitchen to find Tiffany sitting at the table eating some cereal. She noticed that her lunch is ready.

"I see that you packed your lunch." "Yes, I didn't want you to have to do too much when you got up this morning. I even made Angel some oatmeal," Tiffany replies with a smile. "Wow, you did help me out a great deal this morning. Thank you." "It's the least I can do. From now on, I will take the time every morning to try helping you out more." "That would be nice Tiffany. And for this, what do I owe you?" "You can give me an extra few dollars for my allowance every week."

"I knew that this was too good to be true," Sinclair says as they both start laughing. "Tiffany, I want to apologize for what I said to you last night. I mean, I could have said it in a nicer way, but you challenging me made me more upset." "I understand that you were just looking out for my best interest at heart; and for that I respect you." "I'm glad that you understand." "So, I guess, you still don't want me to talk with that homeless man if I see him at school today?" "My answer hasn't changed since last night, Tiffany. Stay away from that man. Promise me that you will." "For a few extra dollars a week added to my allowance, I think I can make that happen."

"I can't believe that I'm getting hustled by my baby sister! Ok, if you promise me that you won't bother that man, you have a deal." "I promise," says Tiffany. After the agreement, Sinclair gets dressed and takes Tiffany and Angel to school and daycare. As they pull up to Tiffany's school, Sinclair reminds her about the deal. "I know, I know," she says while opening the door to get out of the car.

Tiffany goes into the school building for class and Sinclair gets ready to leave. As she is pulling away from the school, she spots the homeless man that Tiffany has been telling her about heading toward the school. "There goes that that man," she says, looking at him, as she drives by. "I hope that the girl will remember what we talked about."

Recess approaches and it's time for the students to go outside for recreation. Tiffany spots the homeless man at the fence of the school's playground. She grabs her book bag and walks towards him. "Hello sir," she says as she reaches into her book bag. "I have something to give you." She pulls out the bag lunch that she made him at home and gives it to him.

The man reaches over the fence and takes the lunch. He quickly opens the bag and begins to eat the food. "Thank you," he says with a large amount of food in his mouth. Tiffany is so amused at how hungry this man must be, given that the food was eaten at a very fast pace. "You haven't eaten anything in a long time, I see. What is your name?" The homeless man looks down at Tiffany with a strange look on his face, very surprised that she is trying to get to know him. "Eric," he responds.

"Why do you come up to this school every day?" "I miss this school." "Why do you miss it?" "A long time ago, I used to teach at this school." "What happened that made you stop teaching?" "When my mother died, I had a really hard time getting over her death and I started using drugs and drinking a lot. This caused me to lose everything that I had, including my teaching job, here, at the school."

"So you come up to the school every day because you miss it?" "Yes, because this is the only place that reminds me of how good I used to have it before I started using drugs. My advice to you is to never in your life use drugs and to stay in school. Sometimes, it gets so bad that I can't remember what I need to do." "Have you been using drugs lately?" "I haven't really because I never have any money to buy them."

Eric gets quiet while he is watching the kids run around and play on the playground. He points out to Tiffany the many different things he used to involve himself with when he would be outside, in charge of supervising the kids. "Do you ever want to teach again?" "If I had the opportunity to teach again, I would jump at the chance. They told me before I was put on suspension that, if I ever quit using drugs and managed to get myself together, they would let me teach again."

"Well, why don't you get yourself together, so that you can have that opportunity again?" "If it was that easy, I would be teaching by now." "If you are serious about teaching again and wanting help, I could help you," she says. "Why would you do that?" "Because you seem like a nice man and everybody deserves a second chance. At least that's what my grandma used to tell me."

"What can you do to help?" says Eric. "Every day that I'm at school, I can bring you a lunch and, on Friday, I can bring some money that my sister gives me to help you. I don't know, maybe you can buy some clothes, so you can change out of the ones you got because they smell really badly," she says while fanning her face because of the odor. Eric laughs back at her.

"If I do this, you have to promise me that you are going to put the money to good use." Eric looks down at Tiffany and reaches his hand through the fence holes to shake her hand in agreement to the deal. "No offense, but I really don't know where your hands have been," she says laughing. "I can respect that." "Well, that's the teacher calling us in now, so I have to go back to my classroom. Remember what we talked about. You have to help yourself if you want other people to help you."

Before Tiffany leaves, he asks her one more a question. "How do you get to be so smart at such a young age, and wise at that? You can't be no more than eleven years old!" "I have learned a lot from my grandma, my uncle Pete and my sister Sinclair." "Those are three great people, I see. They have raised a smart little girl." "Well, I will see you tomorrow. Just remember the deal and you do your part and I promise to do mine."

Tiffany grabs her book bag and runs back towards the school building. One teacher notices that Tiffany has been at the fence talking to the homeless man. "I guess you found a new friend," she observes. "He was hungry and I just gave him something to eat." "That man you were talking to taught here before. He was great teacher. He was actually voted Teacher of the Year at one point."

"When his mother died, he just threw it all away. All he needs is help and he can teach again. Let's hope that he gets the help that he needs." The teacher puts her hand on the back of Tiffany and walks her inside the school. That afternoon, school is out and Sinclair is there to pick up Tiffany. "I saw that homeless man when I dropped you off this morning. Did you happen to see him?" she asks Tiffany, as she is closing the car door.

"Yes, I saw him but I didn't say anything to him, as you told me not to." "Good. I'm glad that you took my advice and decided not to talk to him. It's for your own good," Sinclair explains, as she drives off from the school, on her way to pick up her daughter. "I have something to tell you," Tiffany suddenly says. "What is it?" "Well since we are on the subject of the homeless man, I wasn't the only one that notices him when he started coming tour school." "What do you mean?"

"Well, apparently, he has been coming to the school grounds for quite some time now." "And how do you know that?" "One of my teachers told me today that he once taught at my school a long time ago." "Did she say how long?" "About four years ago." "Why did he stop teaching? Did she tell you that?" "She said that he was one of their best teachers back then. But, when his mom passed away, he started drinking a lot and that caused him to lose his job." "So is that's why he comes up to the school every day!"

"She told me that she talked to him a few times, hoping that it might remind him of the opportunities he is missing in life. She wishes that he would do something with his life, rather than just throwing it all away." Sinclair feels a little sadden about the homeless man story. "Wow! I would have never thought the he was once a teacher." "See, you can't judge a book by its cover." "Well, that's just one homeless man that just happens to be alright. But there are many out there that are crazy and do bad things."

"One day you are going to thank me," Tiffany suddenly says to her. "What's that's supposed to mean?" Tiffany does not answer to Sinclair straight away. "Just because your teacher tells you that this man used to be good, it doesn't mean that I want you to talk to him," she says in a serious tone. "I didn't say that I was going to talk to him. I just said you are going to thank me one day."

"Well, with that comes a motive, and I don't want you to have any kind of motives." "Can we just stop it? I promised you that I wasn't going to talk to Eric and I'm not." Sinclair picks up on Tiffany calling the homeless man by his name. "Did you just call him Eric? How did you know his name?" "My teacher told me. I ask her what his name was and she told me. Is that a problem?" "You don't need to get personal information about that man. You are not going to help him. Do I make myself clear for the last time?" "Ok, no more talks about Mr. Eric," Tiffany replies in a sarcastic tone. "What's for dinner? I'm hungry." "When I pick up Angel we will go out to get something to eat."

Weeks go by and Tiffany has delivered on her promise to help Eric get back on his feet. Every day, she continued to give him packed lunches and, on Fridays, when Sinclair gives her allowance of twenty-five dollars, she would give it all to him. Every week, Tiffany could see some marked changes in Eric. He started wearing better clothes and even had a haircut. He started to look like a regular human being.

Because he wants to teach again, Eric uses some of the money that Tiffany is giving him each week to purchase study materials, so that he can prepare himself for the state's Praxis Exams that he must pass to get certified again. He also uses some of the money to get a room at a local lodge in the city and to catch the bus around the city. Things are starting to look good for a change.

It's time for recess and Tiffany spots Eric at the fence.

"Wow! You look like a different person. I like the new look," she says, referring to his khakis, his brown dress shoes and his burgundy button-down shirt he has on. "You look more like a teacher now." "I feel more like a teacher now. Thanks to you, I can see the vision a little better," he says with a smile. "It's not over until you are actually back in the classroom, teaching again. So, we still have a little way to go, but we are on the right track." "Yes ma'm, pretty little lady," he says to her with a salute.

Tiffany pulls the brown bag out of her book bag. "Here is your lunch. I made something really special this time." He looks into the bag and finds a Big Mac sandwich that she got from McDonalds last night. "Wow, I haven't had a Big Mac in a long time. Thank you." She notices that Eric is carrying his practice exams in his hand. "Here, you are going to need this," she says, handing him her black book bag.

"Look, this is too much. I used to be a teacher and I know how important it is for you to have your book bag. I can't take it." Tiffany pauses for a minute. The bell sounds and she know that she has to go back into the building for her next class. She throws her book bag over the fence to Eric and runs away. As she is running away, she yells to him, "You can't give it back now, it's yours." Eric laughs, as he looks at the book bag on the ground. "That is one special little girl."

He picks up the book bag off the ground and put his materials inside. He walks away from the school, down the sidewalk, eating his Big Mac. That afternoon, Sinclair is there to pick up Tiffany. She notices that Tiffany has her books in her hands and no book bag. "What happened to your book bag?" "I think someone stole my bag." "How could someone still your bag?" Tiffany just looks away and remains silent.

"Don't y'all have lockers to put your things inside? I mean are you using your locker at all times?" "When I went to gym class today, I couldn't find it after the class. I think someone picked it up," she says with a smirk on her face. "Tomorrow, when you go to the class, you make sure that your teachers know about your book bag missing or stolen," says Sinclair with an angry look on her face. "I don't know what I'm going to do with you," She adds, smiling, as they head for home.

Two months have passed by. Eric is preparing himself to take the Praxis Exam. Tiffany sees him again at the school. "Well the big day has come," he says with a huge smile on his face. "What big day?" "Tomorrow, I will be taking the Praxis Exam for my teaching certification. I'm a little nervous, though." "Don't be nervous. You have taken this test before, so I'm pretty sure that you will do a great job." "I sure hope so."

Once again, Tiffany had prepared a lunch for Eric and gives it to him. "You don't have to keep bringing me lunches and giving me money anymore. I have some good news to tell you." She interrupts him. "I promised until you start teaching again that I would do this for you and I'm a girl of my word," she says throwing the bag over the fence. "I do appreciate it, but I now can buy my own food."

Tiffany has a puzzled look on her face. "How are you going to get food if I stop giving you money and bringing you food?" "I am happy to say that I have started working at a restaurant until I start teaching again. I mean, the money is not much, but it helps me pay for a monthly lodge and provides me with money to purchase food." "That's great." "I also have some bad news."

On hearing those words, Tiffany's smile is suddenly replaced by a concerned look on her face. "What's the bad news?" "I don't think that I will be coming back to the school to see you unless I get my teaching job back." "That is bad news, but also good news. I will always know that you are doing well and that's all that matters." "The place that I will be staying at provides me with a phone. If you are able to call me, I can give you my room number, so that we can keep in touch."

"That would be nice," Tiffany says and Eric takes out a pen and a piece of paper and writes his number down. Don't lose this because, once I'm gone from here, this will be the only way to contact me." He reaches through the fence holes and gives Tiffany the paper. "Am I allowed to give you a handshake now?" he asks, laughing. "I don't want to give you any germs." Tiffany reaches through the fence and gives him a firm handshake. "I think the germs are long gone; at least the ones you had before." They both laugh and give each other a final handshake. Eric leaves the school and walks away.

Sinclair is unable to pick Tiffany up from school today, so she calls the school to see if one of her teachers could bring her home. When they arrive at Tiffany's house, Sinclair comes out to greet the teacher and tell thank her for doing her a favor. "That's a great little sister you have." "Thank you," says Sinclair. "Do I owe you anything for bringing her home?" "Not at all; we need more kids like Tiffany." "What do you mean?" "Well every day, Tiffany has been helping one of our old teachers that have been coming up to the school on a regular basis. She would bring him food and sometimes give him a little money from time to time." On hearing that, the look on Sinclair's face revealed great shocked and surprise. "I think she has done a great job helping him get back on his feet because he looks a lot better than before."

After Sinclair tells the teacher 'thank you' and she pulls off, she quickly runs into the house, screaming Tiffany's name very loudly. "So you lied to me. You told me that you were not going to talk to that man." "I wanted to help him, that's all." "When I asked you have you been seeing him, you looked right into my eyes and lied to me." "I'm sorry. I knew that you would get mad at me if I told you that I was helping him, so I didn't tell you the truth. He's a changed man and I helped him with that change."

"I can't even look at you right now. I am so disappointed in you. Go to your room now!" "You are not my mother, you are my sister and you can't tell me what to do!" "Not only am I your sister, I am your legal guardian and you'd better get your room now."

Tiffany storms into her room and slams the door. Sinclair is furious and very upset with Tiffany. Later that night, Sinclair goes to Tiffany's room and knocks on the door. "Tiffany, can I come in?" "If you are going to yell at me some more the answer is 'no'." "I promise that I want yell at you." Tiffany unlocks the door and lets Sinclair in. "Although I am mad at you, I shouldn't have yelled at you. I didn't expect you to lie to me though."

"When we were in Baltimore and Grandma asked you what happened to your neck, you lied to her. In my case, I was trying to help someone. What was your reason for lying to Grandma?" "You have a point, Tiffany." "You said before that if you are lying to spare someone's feelings from being hurt, then that's ok. And I didn't want to hurt your feelings."

"I tell you what, from this day forward, we are going to tell each other the truth, no matter how painful it is. Is that ok with you?" "I think I can handle that. Plus I'm bad at telling lies." Sinclair hugs Tiffany and tells her that she will always love her.

It's November 11, 2000 and it is Tiffany's birthday. She will be turning eleven today. As promised, Sinclair is giving her a birthday party. It is not really a surprise birthday party because Tiffany had been bugging her about it for some weeks now. Sinclair goes to Tiffany's room to wake her up.

"Get up, sleepy head. Rise and shine," she says while pulling back the blinds. "Today is your big day. It's your birthday." Sinclair jumps onto the bed, tickling her to get up. "Stop, stop, that tickles," Tiffany shouts through the laughter. "Ok, how do you want your birthday party to look?" "Since I'm a princess, make it look like Snow White's ball." "You got it."

"Did you invite enough friends from your school?" "I think there will be between twenty to twenty five guests."

"That's a lot." "You can handle it. But I have a confession to make. There's one more person that I want to invite." "And who is that?" Sinclair turns around and stares at Tiffany. "I want to invite that guy Eric who I have been helping." "You mean that homeless man Eric?" "He's not homeless anymore. He has a job and a place to stay now; all because of my help." "So you really want him to come?" "Yes, I think that you should meet him. Since he cleaned himself up, he's not bad looking either."

"Well, in that case, call him up and invite him." "Thank you," Tiffany says and immediately grabs the home phone to call Eric. After a few minutes talking to him on the phone, he agrees to come to her birthday party. The evening comes and the birthday party has started. All the kids are in the back, playing. Sinclair hears a knock at her door. She opens it to find a man standing outside.

"You must be Eric?" "Yes I am." She invites him in. Tiffany comes to the front. "You made it. Thanks for coming." In his hands, he holds a bag that has some presents for Tiffany. "This is for you," he says and gives her the bag. Tiffany looks inside and sees many of her favorite gifts. "How did you know that I liked these things?" "The book bag you gave me had your birthday wish list in it."

Sinclair stares at Tiffany. "So that's where your book bag went." "I have another surprise for you." He goes back outside and comes back in with a new black book bag with an envelope inside. Tiffany takes it out and opens it. "Three hundred dollars, wow!" "What is the money for?" asks

Sinclair, suddenly uneasy about the whole situation. "She has been giving me money every week and that is the amount it totaled to."

"That was very nice of you." "I'd always known that I would pay her back." "I guess I owe you a big 'thank you'." "All the thanks go to Tiffany. There is still one more piece of good news I wish to share with you, Tiffany." "What is it?" Tiffany shouts impatient to know. "I got my teacher's certificate. I can teach again." Tiffany runs up and gives him a hug. "I told you that you could do it!" Sinclair stares at Eric and is very amazed to see a man that overcame adversity. "Thank you for being such a great friend to Tiffany," she tells him, fighting tears of pure joy.

CHAPTER 12

It's been a week since Tiffany's birthday party and Sinclair and Eric have been conversing on a daily basis. Things seem to be going great between the two of them. One weekend, Eric asks Sinclair out. "I was wondering if you were free this weekend; maybe you could let me take you out." "I don't know. I don't have anybody to watch my daughter and Tiffany." "Tiffany is a smart and intelligent girl. I'm pretty sure she can watch your daughter for you." "I don't like that idea. I wouldn't feel comfortable leaving them alone in the house while I'm out."

Eric gets quiet, trying to come up with other ideas, so that he could take Sinclair out. "I have an idea," he finally says. "How about we hook up early in the day and bring both your daughter and Tiffany with us. We can go someplace fun, where they will enjoy themselves." "That sounds great and all, but I don't think it's a good idea for me to bring my daughter to a date. I don't want it look like we are on a family outing or anything," says Sinclair, with a slight laughter.

"Do you have any friends that will look after them?" When Eric mentioned friends, Sinclair begins to think about Christy and Jana and about how it really would have helped her out a lot if they were still friends with each other. "My friends and I fell out a couple of years ago, so it's just me now. I haven't met any new friends since then." "Well, I don't have any other ideas I can come up with, so maybe we just have to be phone friends," Eric says with a laugh. "Who knows, maybe one day, we will have the opportunity to see each other."

After Sinclair gets off the phone with Eric, she goes into the living room where Tiffany is playing with Angel. "You were on the phone for quite some time," Tiffany notes, giving her a knowing look. "So, is that a problem?" "Not at all; it's just at one point, Eric was this homeless man that you didn't want me around, but now you seem to like him. I told you that he was a good person." "Ok, maybe I shouldn't have put him in the same category as everyone else, but you still have to be careful with people and get to know them first."

"As they say, never judge a book by its cover," Tiffany says with a smile. "I guess I owe you an apology. He really did turn out to be a great person thus far." "So are you going to see him soon?" "Well, it's funny that you should mention that, as he wants to take me out tonight, but I turned him down, as I don't have anybody to watch y'all while I'm out."

Sinclair looks down at Tiffany, who is lying on the floor with a distrusted look on her face. "What, you don't think that I can watch Angel while you are gone?" "It's not that I don't trust you, it's just that you are not old enough for me to leave you here alone with her." "Not old enough?" Tiffany retorts, as she gets up from the floor and stands in front of Sinclair. "Excuse me, but I just turned eleven years old last week, thank you very much," she says while rolling her eyes in the back of her head, moving her finger from side to side.

Sinclair laughs at the funny faces Tiffany is making. "Plus, Angel is my niece and I can and will do a great job watching her." "Let me think about it." Sinclair ponders on the idea of letting Tiffany babysit, so she can go out with Eric.

About five minutes later, she comes back into the living room. "Ok, if I let you do this, you have to promise me that you will follow all the rules that I am going to give you." "I promise. What are the rules?" Tiffany gets up again from the floor and sits next to Sinclair on the sofa. "Rule number one; don't answer the door or let anybody in while I'm gone. Rule number two; if anything goes wrong, you call me immediately." "Is that all?" "Yes that's basically it." "I can handle that. You just go in your room and call Eric so y'all can go out."

Sinclair rushes in her room feeling good about the idea that Tiffany is responsible enough to babysit. She call Eric back. "I have some good news. Tiffany convinced me to trust her to watch Angel. I guess I'm free after all." "That's great." "So, what time are you picking me up?" she asks. Eric pauses for a minute. "Well, to be honest, it's going to be pretty hard for me to pick you up." "Why is that?" "Remember, I was homeless and I don't think that homeless people have cars," he says and they share a laugh.

"I am so sorry. I keep forgetting that you were once this unfortunate man." "Nice way to put it." "Well, if you will tell me where you are staying, I can come to pick you up." Eric gives Sinclair the address, along with the directions and she agrees to come and get him. "You forgot to tell me what time to come get you." "Well, since Tiffany is going to be alone at home, I think it is best that we hook up early in the day, so that you can get back home."

"How nice of you," Sinclair says with a smile and, after setting the time, hangs up the phone. She starts preparing for the evening. As it's been a long time since she has been out, Sinclair has no clue what to wear and asks Tiffany to come into the room to assist her. "What do you think I should wear?" Sinclair lays a black dress, jeans and a black sweater on the bed. "So what do you think?" she asks Tiffany.

"Well it's kind of cold outside. I think you should wear those jeans with the black sweater and your black boots. You don't want to look to desperate and that might be the impression you would make with that tight dress on," she says, laughing. "You have to remember that he was homeless, so I don't think he have to many clothes himself. So just dress casually and let it be." "I can't believe that I am getting schooled by my little sister." "By the way, big sis, you know that I'm looking for a little compensation for babysitting."

"You mean to tell me that I have to pay you to watch Angel for me?" "Hey, this is a business and I'm sure pay comes with the business." They both laugh and Sinclair offers Tiffany to add ten dollars to her allowance next week. "I don't mind you charging me. It lets me know that my baby sister is trying to be independent."

Tiffany leaves Sinclair's room and goes back into the front, where Angel is playing with her toys. Sinclair hops into the shower. She then puts on her clothes, does her hair and makeup and is ready for her date. "Well Tiffany, I am ready to go." She picks Angel up, gives her a hug and a kiss, tells them 'bye' and leaves the house.

Soon, she arrives at the motel lodge to pick Eric up. He is already waiting outside and gets in the car. "Wow, you look and smell great!" he compliments her. "You don't look bad yourself," Sinclair replies as he observed Eric, who has on some dark blue jeans with a cream sweater. "So, where should we go?" he asks. "Well, I am a little hungry, so maybe we can go to a restaurant I went to when I first moved down here." "And what restaurant is that?" "The Cheesecake Factory," she says.

Once they reach the restaurant, a valet approaches them and offers to park the car. Eric and Sinclair exit and he opens the door to the restaurant for her. Soon, they are seated by the hostess. "The last time I was in here was when my friend Christy and my ex boyfriend Derrick were here." "Why haven't you been back here since then?" "Well a lot has happened in that time and we all went our separate ways."

"When you say that a lot has happened, what exactly do you mean?" "Do you really want to know?" "Yes, I want to know everything about you," he says with a smile on his face. "Well Derrick, my ex, cheated on me with my best friend Christy. My friend Jana met this guy Jerome, who apparently convinced her to work for him as a stripper. As for me, I had a baby within that time frame and our lives were no longer compatible, I guess." "Wow that's a lot," Eric replies, not knowing what else to say. "So, I really never talked to my friends again. I simply couldn't, given all the stuff that happened."

After they spend a few more minutes talking, the waitress comes and takes their order. Once they are alone again, the conversation starts up again. "So your daughter—" Sinclair quickly cuts him off. "What about my daughter?" "Where is her father? Is he still around?" "I have no idea where her father is." Sinclair gets a little edgy when Eric asks her about Angel's father.

"I'm sorry to have made you feel uncomfortable by mentioning the whereabouts of her father." "It's not your fault. It's just that something horrible happened to me a couple of years ago and I still think about it." Sinclair takes a sip of water. "Enough about me, do you have kids?" "I have no kids and have never been married. It's just me, all by myself." "Do you want a wife and kids one day?" "Of course I do. I can't wait to have a child one day."

"Do you have any pictures of your daughter with you?" Eric asks, taking a sip from his glass. "If you do, I would love to see some." Sinclair goes into her purse and pulls out several pictures of Angel. She hands Eric a couple of photos. He takes the pictures and stares at them for quite some time. "What's wrong?" "I'm speechless. She is beautiful." "That's my Angel," Sinclair says with a smile. "Why did you name her Angel?"

Sinclair pauses for a moment. "I named her Angel because she came into this world under some unfortunate circumstances." "What do you mean by that, if you don't mind me asking?" "Let's just say it wasn't a planned pregnancy. So,

I assumed that it was a gift from God and that he sent me one of is angels to take care of. Let's also say that her father is missing out on a great little girl."

Eric looks at the pictures some more with a puzzled look on his face. "Why are you looking like that?" "I'm just amazed at how much she reminds me of my mother." "Is that so?" "Yes," he says. "Your mother must be a beautiful woman." Eric laughs at that comment. "I'm just looking at her cheekbones and her eyes and I swear, it as if I'm looking at my mother."

Sinclair gets very quiet as Eric looks at the pictures of Angel. "Is there anything else that you see that reminds you of anybody else?" Eric thinks hard. "Oh yeah, I remember seeing some old photos of my grandmother and she has the same curly hair that your daughter has." "Wow, I guess my daughter can fit right in with your family," Sinclair says with a smile, even though she is rather concerned by the news.

"Any man would love to have your daughter with him. She seems adorable." Eric is about to say more, but the waitress brings their food to the table. Sinclair and Eric start to eat their food in silence. He suddenly notices a scar on her neck. "May I ask you what happened to your neck?" Sinclair looks up at him, pain in her eyes. She quietly places her fork back onto her plate before responding, "You are asking a lot of questions." "I'm sorry, but I just couldn't help but notice the mark on your neck." "You sound just like my grandma and Tiffany, questioning me about my neck."

Sinclair starts to reflect on the night she was raped. "Are you ok?" Sinclair is in a daze and doesn't respond. "I'm sorry to have made you feel uncomfortable." "No it's not you. I've just had a hard time getting over what I'd been through a couple of years ago." "So, I guess, you are not going to tell me what happened to you?" "When the time is right, I will be more than happy to fill you in on what I've been through besides what I told you so far. But since this is our first date, I don't think we should be getting so deep into personal matters."

Eric picks up the pictures again and looks at them. "Man, there is something about this girl," he says to himself. "Ok, enough with the photos!" Sinclair grabs the pictures from Eric and they continue with their dinner.

Afterwards, they get back into the car and Sinclair drives Eric home. "I really had a great time today," he says. "I've enjoyed myself as well." Sinclair pulls up at the lodge where Eric is staying to drop him off. He gets out of the car, walks around to the driver's side and opens her door. He reaches out his hand and asks her to get out.

"I would like to get a 'goodbye' hug before you leave." Sinclair is flattered. She gets out of the car and gives him a hug. He whispers in her ear, "So, did I pass the test?" "You passed the test when you made my sister happy." He squeezes her tightly and kisses her on the cheek. He reopens the door for her and Sinclair gets back into her car. "I will call you when I make it home." "Please do," he responds.

Sinclair drives off. As she is leaving for home, she grabs one of the photos that Eric was looking at. "I wonder why he said that Angel reminded him of his mother so many times."

She then reflects back on that night of her rape. She thinks about how she was held that day and compares it to how she was held by Eric just moments ago. She then looks back at the photo of her daughter and then pictures Eric's appearance in her head.

She thinks of his nice curly hair and his light brown eyes. "It wasn't the fact that he was looking at Angel's photos, it was how he was looking at them as if he had seen a ghost," she says to herself. Sinclair starts to assume things. She thinks of him being homeless and the way he was looking at Angel's photos. "No it can't be," she says aloud, referring to Eric being the father of her daughter and the man that raped her two years ago.

She gets home and goes inside to a warm welcome from her daughter and Tiffany. "So how did it go?" "It was quite interesting; especially at the end of the date." "What do you mean?" "It started to feel a little strange, that's all." "Did he do anything wrong?" "As far as the date goes, no, but he may be responsible for something else. It's a possibility."

Sinclair starts getting Angel ready for bed but can't get the thought of Eric being the homeless man that attacked her off her mind. After she gets Angel ready for bed and then check on Tiffany, she calls Eric. "Hey, sorry it took me so long to call you, but I wanted to get my daughter ready for bed." "That's not a problem at all. Your daughter should always come first." "Thanks for understanding."

Eric notices that Sinclair is very quiet on the phone, something that he's not used to from the many conversations that they had on the phone before. "Is everything ok?" he asks. "You are very quiet." "Well, I just started thinking about our date." "What about it made you so quiet?" he asks. Sinclair hesitates before answering, "Just some things that has happened to me. I'm just trying to put them all together."

"Does this concern me?" Eric asks, and Sinclair wants to say yes, but doesn't want to accuse him of something she cannot prove. She knows that, based on him looking at Angel's photos with interest, she cannot assume that Eric had anything to do with what happened to her two years ago. "No, this doesn't concern you." "Well, if I can help you with anything you let me know." Sinclair thinks of how to put the pieces together. "Are you free next week?" "I should be," he says. "Maybe we can get together and have a drink." "That would be nice." Sinclair plans another date with Eric but has something else in mind. They arrange their date and get off the phone.

The following weekend approaches and Sinclair is out to prove if there is a connection between Eric and Angel. She gets into her car and goes over to his motel lodge. "I couldn't wait to see you," he says, as he opens the door to let Sinclair in. The evening begins with Eric opening a bottle of wine and ordering some takeout. They eat and drink for the next couple of hours.

Sinclair recalls that night when describing the suspect to the police. She remembers telling them that her attacker had a keloid cut on his neck. She tries to figure out how she can see if Eric has that mark on his neck. She curses herself for not paying attention to his neck the day she met him for the first time at Tiffany's birthday party or last week, when they went out.

She then comes up with an idea to see if he, indeed, was her attacker. She begins to seduce him. "Hey, let's lay on the bed," she tells him. She lies on the bed and he joins her. She starts kissing him. "How about you take that hoodie off, so that we can get a little more comfortable?" she asks seductively. Eric obliges and Sinclair rolls on top of him, kissing him all the while. Unfortunately, she sees the mark on his neck and jumps up very quickly. "What's wrong?" he asks, shocked at her sudden change of mood. "You stay right there," she shouts.

"It was you," she says, as tears start running down her face. "It was me what?" "Remember you asked me about my baby's father and I didn't tell you. It was because I was raped by a homeless man two years ago and it was you." "What?" yells Eric. "Why would I do such a thing?" "It is no surprise that my daughter looks like your mother, since you are her father."

Eric, confused look on his face, sits on the bed. "If I really did that to you, I must have really been out of my mind and was on some serious drugs." He looks back up at Sinclair. "If it was me, I am sorry to have hurt you and made your life difficult." Sinclair cries out even louder. Eric comes over to try and comfort her.

"Don't touch me! Don't ever put your hands on me!" Eric backs away from her. "I want to know if she is really my daughter and, if so, I will take care of my responsibilities." Sinclair looks at him with a disgusted look on her face. "I don't want you near me or my baby. If she is yours, you'd better believe that you will never see her."

Sinclair runs out of his motel lodge into her car and goes back home. "I can't believe that I went out with the man that raped me," she says to herself. She gets home and Tiffany immediately notices that she has been crying. "What happened to you?" Without replying, Sinclair picks up Angel and holds her tightly. "I am so sorry baby. Mommy will never let anything happen to you, I promise," she says while hugging Angel tightly. "Sinclair, you are scaring me." "I'm sorry, Tiffany, but there is something that I have to tell you about Eric."

"What about Eric?" "Remember when I told you and Grandma that lie about my neck? Well, I am going to tell you the truth now." She sits down with her baby in her arms. "I was raped by this homeless man two years ago when I was volunteering at this shelter." Tiffany sits back into the couch, shocked by this revelation. "What does this have to do with Eric?" "Eric was the homeless man that raped me. He is also Angel's father."

Tiffany jumps up. "You are a liar! He would never do anything like that." "Tiffany, that's why I didn't want you to mess with a homeless man because I was afraid for you and didn't want anything to happen to you," she says. "How do you know that the man that did that to you was Eric?" "The guy that did it had the same mark on his neck that Eric has. At dinner last week, he kept saying how much Angel reminded him of his mother. When he said that, I put all the pieces together and realized that it was him."

Tiffany begins to cry. "I'm sorry, Tiffany. I know how much you cared for Eric, but we just can't see him anymore." Tiffany runs into her room and slams the door. She picks up the phone and calls Eric. He answers the phone, thinking that it's Sinclair. "Sinclair," he calls her name. "This is not Sinclair, this is Tiffany."

"Tiffany, your sister said that I did a bad thing to her a couple of years ago and, if I did, I am really, really sorry." "I don't want you calling my sister or our house again." Tiffany yells at him and slams the phone down hard. She then goes back into the front to sit with Sinclair.

"I'm sorry that this happened to you, sis. He won't bother you again." Tiffany gives Sinclair a hug. The next morning, Sinclair calls her grandma to tell her the truth about what really happened to her. "Hey Grandma, how's everything going with you?" "I'm hanging in there baby," she says with a smile. "How are my three best people in the world are doing?" "Besides what I have to tell you, we are doing a little better." "What is it that you have to tell me?" Grandma asks, curious to hear the news.

"I just want to tell you about what happened to me two years ago, even though I should've really told you the truth then." "Let me brace myself before you spill your guts." "I lied to you about my neck and how the mark got there. In truth, one night, when I was volunteering at the homeless shelter two days before Thanksgiving, I was attacked and raped by a homeless man. That is how I got pregnant with Angel."

"Oh dear, I am sorry to learn that something so horrible happened to you. What hurts even more is that you had to go through that alone, as you never told me." "I'm sorry that I lied to you Grandma. I didn't want you to worry about me and at that time, as Uncle Pete had just died. It was just too much going on at that time." "I understand, baby. Since you are being honest with me, I have to be honest with you too." "What are you talking about Grandma?" "I have to tell you the truth about your mother and father."

Sinclair gets very silent, bracing herself for something unpleasant. "The same thing that happened to you happened to your mother. She was raped and got pregnant with you." Grandma can hear Sinclair crying through the phone. "She did die because of the drug use, but she was raped and had you."

"What about my father? Where is he?" Grandma pauses before she answers. "We just buried him two years ago today." "What are you saying Grandma?" "I'm saying that your father was Uncle Pete." Sinclair jumps up and screams no out loud. "Why did y'all keep this from me for this long?" "Your mom and Uncle Pete had just met and he too was using drugs."

"One night, he was so high that he attacked your mother and raped her. I am sure that it was due to the effects of the drugs that he did such a thing. So, after a while, your mother forgave him and she chose to keep you." Sinclair is very shocked to hear the news. "Your mom was so hooked on drugs, as was as Uncle Pete, that I took you in. When your mom died, as you noticed, Uncle Pete kept coming around. He felt as that it would be better that you assumed that he was your uncle rather than your father, simply because he felt that he was a disappointment to you."

"I can't believe that the man I called my uncle all my life was actually my dad," Sinclair says. "What about Tiffany's father?" she asks. "Tiffany's father is somewhere in Baltimore, but the only man she has ever had in her life was Uncle Pete. "What should I do, Grandma? Should Angel know who her father is?" "It's up to you. Still, if I were you, I would forgive him for what he has done and look at the change in him. If he was unaware of his actions due to him being on drugs, then maybe he does deserve another chance." Sinclair thinks about what Grandma is saying very carefully. "Maybe I should think about giving my friends another chance as well," she adds.

After Sinclair gets off the phone with Grandma, she ponders about the decisions she has to make. Finally, she picks up her cell phone and strolls down to Christy's number she got from Derrick at the mall. She makes the call and Christy answers immediately.

"Oh my God, is this you Sinclair?" Christy screams. "Yes it is," Sinclair replies nervously."I can't believe that I am actually on the phone with you. I thought I would never see you again." "I'm happy to hear your voice as well." "So what have you been up to?" asks Christy. "To be honest, girl, we would be on this phone all day if I chose to tell you everything that has happened over the past two years." "Well, we need to find a time, so that we can talk," Christy says with a smile.

"How did you get my number?" she asks, remembering that her number had changed. "I ran into Derrick at the mall about a month ago. He gave me your number and insisted that I call you." "Did he tell you anything else?" "No, not really. We didn't talk for too long." Christy gets a little quiet. "What was he supposed to tell me?" asks Sinclair. "Never mind, I guess I will tell you when I see you again." "Well, I have bought a house and I never really had a chance to have a housewarming party. So, how about you and Jana come over to my place next weekend, so we can catch up on some things."

"That sounds like a great idea. I will call Jana up and we will come. It will be like old times." "One more thing, Christy; I just want to say that I am sorry for what happened between us. Derrick told me about that day and I all I can say that should have believed my friend over some man." "Apology accepted." "Well, I guess, I will see y'all next weekend." "You bet," says Christy.

Eric crosses Sinclair's mind. She can't deny that she cares for him. She also can't forget about what he has done to her. Still, she knows that Angel needs to know who her father is. She calls Eric. "I never thought that I would hear from you again," he says when he picks up the phone. "I'm just calling to see if you would like to see your daughter." "I would love to see her," he says sincerely.

Sinclair promises that she will bring Angel over to the lodge to see Eric. Eric is so excited that, every few minutes, he is looking outside of his window to see if she pulled up yet. Sinclair finally arrives. Before they could get upstairs, Eric runs quickly downstairs. He stares at Angel. "Can I hold her?" "She's yours, so I guess so." Sinclair hands over Angel to Eric and the little girl seems very acceptant of him, as she begins to play with him.

"Daddy," Angel suddenly says. Sinclair looks with a sudden shock on her face. "That's right, I'm daddy," Eric says proudly, his voice full of emotion. "So, what now? How often do I get to see her?" "Look, we have to take it one day at a time. We can't move too quickly. Maybe we will start out once or twice a week and then we will go from there." "Anytime is better than no time at all," he says as he is throwing Angel up into the air.

"So what about you and me?" he asks. "I don't think that it will be 'me and you', but for the sake of the baby, we can remain friends." "Anything is better than nothing at all. I also want you to know that what I did to you two years ago wasn't really me. I wasn't in my right frame of mind. I was on something that I never want to involve myself with again." Sinclair begins to trust Eric again. "I am having my friends over at my place next weekend. If you would like to come, you are welcome." "I would love to come."

After about a couple of hours spending time at Eric's place, Sinclair and Angel are heading back home. Tiffany sees them pulling back into the yard. "Where did y'all go?" she asks, opening the front door for them. "I took her to see Eric." "Why did you do that?" "I talked with Grandma and she made me think about some things. I never really had my father in my life and I don't want Angel to not know her father."

"What about what he did to you?" "Sometimes, you have to forgive people for what they do. He seems really hurt for what he has done to me and, for that, I forgive him." "I guess I can forgive him as well." Tiffany picks up the phone to call Eric but Sinclair stops her. "I have a better idea; how about you tell him face to face next weekend." "Why next weekend?" she asks. "Because I am having a party and I invited him, Christy and Jana to come over next weekend."

"Wow! This will be like old times again. I am so happy," Tiffany yells happily. Sinclair walks into the kitchen, but something is going through her mind that is bothering her. She thinks about what Tiffany had just said, about being like old times. "It won't be like old times if Grandma isn't here," she says to herself. She picks up the phone and calls Grandma. "Hey Grandma, I was wondering if you would like to take a trip somewhere next weekend." "What are you up to?" Grandma asks. "Well, you never had a chance to see your great granddaughter and I was wondering if you would like to come visit us next weekend." Grandma thinks about it for a minute. "Yes, I would love to come.

The weekend has arrived and Sinclair is getting everything together. She is very excited about seeing her friends and her grandma. "I can't wait to see Grandma," says Tiffany. "I have to go to the airport to pick her up," says Sinclair, as she grabs her keys, gets Angel, and Tiffany and they pile up into the car. They are soon on their way to the airport. Once there, they see Grandma sitting outside.

They pull up and, as soon as they get out the car, Tiffany runs towards Grandma, with Sinclair, carrying Angel, following close behind. They all give Grandma a warm hug. "Is this my little great grandbaby?" she says with a smile. "She is adorable." Sinclair grabs her bags, puts them into the truck of the car and they leave for home. When they pull up to the house, they notice two cars parked in the yard.

"That's Christy and Jana," says Tiffany. "Who are those little girls they have with them?" "I don't know, but we are going to find out." They park the car and go into the yard. Sinclair, Christy and Jana all run up to each other, screaming for joy. They are extremely happy to see each other. "Who are these two pretty little girls y'all have with y'all?"

Sinclair squats down on one knee to look at the girls. "Those two little girls belong to me and Jana," says Christy. Sinclair is shocked to know that her friends have also given birth to girls. Sinclair calls Tiffany over to bring Angel over to meet the girls. "Is this your baby?" Jana asks. "Yes it is." "We really need to catch up on some things! But first, we need to get out of this cold air."

They all gather their things, go into the house and take a seat in the living room. "Well, who is first to give their testimony?" asks Sinclair. Christy stands up. She looks at Sinclair. "This is my daughter and her name is Sasha. Derrick is her father." The room gets quiet, as everybody assumes that

Sinclair will get upset. "I am happy for you, Christy. Congratulations," says Sinclair, as she jumps up to give her a hug.

Jana stands up next. "This is my daughter." Before she could say who the father was, there's a knock at the door. Sinclair goes to the door and opens it. "Jerome," she says. "What are you doing here?" Jana runs over to Sinclair at the door. "I told him to come. I hope that's ok with you." "That's fine," Sinclair reassures her.

She opens the door for Jerome and lets him in. Jana finishes giving her testimony. "As I was saying, this is my daughter Zuri, and Jerome is her father. We are also engaged." Sinclair offers her congratulations once again and everybody applauds Jana's engagement with Jerome. "So I guess it's your turn, Sinclair," says Jana as she takes a seat.

Sinclair stands up in the middle of the living room. "Well, so much has happened that I can tell y'all all of it now, but I will give y'all the basics. I have been through a lot during the past couple of years and I'm pretty sure y'all have as well. All I have to say is that this is my daughter Angel and her father will be on his way over here soon." Grandma stands up and interrupts Sinclair. "I just want to say a few words. I have raised pretty much all three of you girls and I have seen the growth in y'all. We all make mistakes. You learn from your mistakes and you move on."

Silence envelopes the room, interrupted only by the happy sounds the three little girls are making, as they play in the room. Grandma continues, "What y'all need to learn from this is that mistakes are only temporary, but friendship can last a lifetime. Whenever you are faced with adversity, that's the time when you need to come together. Know that once you break through the hardships of life we call a concrete, a beautiful rose will emerge."

After Grandma gives her speech, there's another knock at the door. This time Tiffany runs over to open the door. "It's Eric," she yells. She opens the door for him and lets him in. "Everybody, I want y'all to meet Eric. This is the father of my daughter." Everybody greets him and Christy and Jana congratulate Sinclair. Tiffany stands up in the middle of the living room. "My turn, my turn! I want to give my testimony."

Everybody is at attention, wanting to hear what she has to say. "I remember, back in Baltimore, when you, Grandma, gave Sinclair a graduation party. Today feels like that day again. And that is why I want to play something." Tiffany runs over to the stereo and a "Celebration" by Kool and the Gang starts to play. They all jump up and sing the words of the song. As they are dancing and singing, Eric pulls Sinclair aside.

"I have been thinking about what I have done." "That's in the past. Let the past be the past," she says. "I can't live with myself knowing what I've done." "What are you trying to tell me Eric?" "What I am trying to say is that what I did it wasn't right. I have decided to turn myself in." He gives Sinclair a hug, kisses Angel and walks out of the house.

The stereo continues to play "Celebration", as Sinclair stands in the door, watching Eric leave. She begins to reflect on everything that she had been through in the past two years. She thinks about Kenneth, Uncle Pete, and recalls the time when Christy, Jana and she were at the Pool Hall that night. As her thoughts move onto Derrick, Tiffany and Grandma, she begins to smile. Once Eric is no longer in sight, she closes the door and leans against the wall. She stares at her friends and family dancing and singing to the tune of the music.

"I have everything I need right in front of me," she says. "I may have lost the battle, but I won the war. I guess the past two years symbolizes that concrete we were trying to break through and now, after many obstacles Christy, Jana and I have been through, we now stand as three proud, beautiful roses." Sinclair walks over and joins her family and friends.

THE END

Thank you from the Author

I'd like to thank you for purchasing my novel. I hope my imagination and message was able to come off clear in your mind. Please feel free to contact me via web so I can hear your thoughts and receive feedback from you.

Again, Thank you.

The website address is, www.DTaylorbooks.com

www.ingramcontent.com/pod-product-compliance
Lightning Source LLC
Chambersburg PA
CBHW020507120726
47904CB00003B/737